Betraying

The Pack

Pack #2

Eve Langlais

New York Times Bestselling Author

Copyright © September 2011, Eve Langlais
Copyright © 2nd Edition April 2016
Cover art © Mina Carter, September 2011/March 2016
2nd Edition Edits by Devin Govaere

Produced in Canada
Published by Eve Langlais
1606 Main Street, PO Box 151
Stittsville, Ontario, Canada, K2S1A3
http://www.EveLanglais.com

ISBN-13: 978 1988 328 26 3

ALL RIGHTS RESERVED

Betraying the Pack is a work of fiction and the characters, events and dialogue found within the story are of the author's imagination and are not to be construed as real. Any resemblance to actual events or persons, either living or deceased, is completely coincidental.

No part of this book may be reproduced or shared in any form or by any means, electronic or mechanical, including but not limited to digital copying, file sharing, audio recording, email and printing without permission in writing from the author.

Prologue

Fear gripped her so tightly she couldn't scream. Heck, she could barely breathe with that *thing* approaching her.

This must be a nightmare.

What else could explain the towering, gaunt creature that approached her with its facsimile of humanity and glowing red eyes. Where else but from the dark depths of her fearful subconscious could a monster with fangs and such a cruel smile exist?

"You're not real," she muttered, her tone unsure and wavering in the dank air of the cement-block cell. She turned her head, refusing to stare at the smirking monstrosity that glided toward her with unseemly grace.

However, taking in the scene around her didn't do anything to reassure her already shot nerves.

Like a scene from a horror movie, she found herself manacled to a wall, her arms stretched up over her head, drawing her up on tiptoe and forcing her muscles to strain. Naked limbs meant the chill air of the room rolled over her helpless body, raising bumps on her skin and tightening her nipples in fear.

The room she hung in appeared like a jail cell,

with gray walls and a heavy door containing one small barred window. Worse than the putrid stench, which she tasted with each inhalation, more frightening than the sense of decay and the chokingly thick dust, but not as frightening as the creature in the room with her, were the moans and gibbering cries she could hear. The pitiful sounds, full of abject misery—and madness—wafted through the partially open door, causing her to shiver. *Will I sound like that once he's done with me?*

She could delude herself all she wanted that she would wake from this nightmare. That such a horrific scenario could not exist. Another part of her knew better. A part of her already screamed in her mind.

The monster halted before her, a creature she clenched her eyes tightly against as she tried so hard to pretend he did not exist. A futile wish.

Fingers tipped with long claws grasped her chin in a painful vise, the sharp points digging into her skin. A whimpering cry escaped her.

"Open your eyes." The words, whispered across her face, clung to her skin like a tenebrous spider web.

"Now." The force of his command invaded her, touched her mind, and even though she didn't mean them to, her eyes opened and fixed upon him. Then, despite herself, she could not look away.

Up close, she could see every detail, from his hair gone silver with only passing streaks of ebony to his face creased and lined with age. But it was his eyes that frightened her most. They shone a ruby red, inhumanly so. Evil was all she could think of. She gazed upon true evil.

His voice, when he finally spoke, emerged low and smooth with a gravelly undertone. "Despite what you keep telling yourself, as you can see, I'm very real. Not perhaps alive by any sense of the human definition, but definitely a force to be reckoned with."

"What are you?" The question whispered from her lips, but she discovered she didn't truly want to know. Didn't want to believe something like *him* could exist.

"I am everything, king, master, and god. Once a Lycan, now also a vampire, I am unique and more powerful than anything this world has known."

And certainly conceited, her hysterical mind thought. Face to face with a myth, she couldn't deny his existence, although she longed to with all her might. "What do you want with me?"

A cruel smile tilted his lips, and the molten glow of his eyes darkened. The red pinpoints bored into her like lasers. "Oh, you are going to do a lot of things for me, Bailey."

He knew her name. For some reason this made her terror ramp up to a higher level. She tried to rationalize that he must have gotten it from her wallet in her purse or overheard it somehow when he'd kidnapped her. However, the forcefulness of his stare and the pulsing pain in her head told her that he'd acquired his knowledge from another source, her mind, torn it from her psyche along with untold other secrets.

"Dear Lord, help me."

A low laugh spilled from the monster, made more chilling by its lack of actual humor. "There is no help for you, Bailey."

"My family—"

"Is gone," he interjected. "Don't you understand yet? I know you, dear Bailey. I've been watching you. Waiting for you. You have no secrets from me. Let me see . . . orphaned only last year. Recently single after your boyfriend took up with your best friend. Such a lonely, desperate girl. No one left to love you. No one to notice you're gone. What a sad, pathetic human you are."

Tears rolled down her cheeks at his bleak assessment of her life. Less a life than a tale of depression.

The creature inhaled deeply. "Ah, the sweet smell of misery. You truly do tempt me to taste your essence. To drain every drop of your blood until you pass into oblivion."

"So do it," she replied, her voice lackluster. Perhaps she could hope for a quick death and avoid the hopelessness she heard echoing about her.

"Such a tease. If I didn't have other uses for you, I would. But fear not, if my plans don't come to fruition, then you will feed me. Perhaps, I'll even let you live long enough that my troops might partake of your flesh. Those brutes are ever rough with the playmates I bring to them. Always requiring fresh pussy."

Bailey couldn't misunderstand his meaning, and her lips trembled as the tears flowed unchecked down her cheeks.

"Pleasant as our chat has been, it's now time to introduce you to your destiny. I've searched long and hard for you, dear Bailey. The voices you hear all around are those who've come before and failed. But you . . . you are different than those other girls. With you, I shall succeed and thus forge ahead with my plans. I warn you, though. The transformation from your mediocre humanity will most definitely hurt, so feel free to scream. Actually, I insist."

Bailey did wail, not to please him but because she had no choice. The liquid agony he poured into her veins proved excruciating beyond anything she could have ever imagined.

However, her living nightmare had only just begun.

Chapter One

Twenty-four hours earlier

Bailey looked around her one-bedroom apartment and sighed. Friday night, and once again, she found herself alone. And not just alone but without even a television for entertainment because hers had decided to die after a bright burst of light on the screen shrank until only a black reflective surface stared back at her. Replacing it at eight thirty on a Friday seemed foolish—and piteous. However, without it to numb her mind, exactly what would she do with the rest of her evening? The thought of reading didn't appeal, and neither did going to bed or staring at her wall.

I could go see a movie. Alone? That seemed too pathetic even for her.

Just a month ago, none of this would have required any thought. She'd have either spent the evening with her boyfriend, Tom, or called her girlfriend Becky to go out. Not anymore, although chances were Tom and Becky were hanging out—together. The two-timing jerks.

The discovery they'd gotten involved and lied to her—and probably also laughed at her ignorance while cavorting naked in her bed, on her sheets, sheets that she'd burned—still hurt. Add to that the death of her parents in a car crash the year before and it was devastating.

But most of all, lonely.

All she currently had to occupy her mind and time was her work. Boring, mind-numbing employment as a call-center operator for a furniture store. Worse, she didn't even have an office to go to or other employees to fraternize with or befriend. Working from home, which used to seem such a boon, was now its own form of prison, as she didn't get the chance to meet people.

And that's not going to change unless I do something about it. She needed to stop wallowing in self-pity. Stop waiting for life, love, and friendship to come knocking on her door—because apparently that plan wasn't working or destiny had lost her address. She yearned for change, a new life, and it needed to start tonight, that very minute.

Time to get on with living and get back on that damned horse called socialization.

Instead of bemoaning her fate over a gallon of ice cream—cookie dough winning top spot—she was going to get dressed in her tightest jeans—tight more because of the pounds she'd put on than design—her prettiest blouse, and cute little boots that she had paid too much for. She would go for a drink, maybe two, and some dancing. She might not find her next BFF at a bar, but damn it, at least she could get out and meet other people, pretend she had a life.

Decided, she prepared herself, slapping on a light coating of makeup, brushing her curly dark hair until it crackled, and dabbing a light perfume behind her ears. All the time she prepared, a chant ran through her head, a pep talk that would have worked better with pom-poms: *You can do this. People go out and make friends every day. You can do this.* She hoped.

Grabbing her cordless phone, she called a cab, not foolish enough to walk around alone even at this early time of night. As she exited her apartment, locking it behind her, she caught a furtive movement at the end of the hall by the stairs. She took a step in that direction, straining to see if someone hid there, ready to scream if there was. Her paranoia had basis.

Just two weeks ago, and only a few blocks away, a young woman had been abducted and her apartment ransacked. Worse, the cops never caught the guy. Caution had become her middle name since that crime.

Craning on tiptoe, she stared hard at the semi-reflective window of the stairwell, wondering if she'd finally let paranoia take over. She saw nothing, and yet, she still took a step back, the certainty that someone hid there increasing despite a lack of evidence. *Danger*, whispered a voice in her mind. *Run.*

The ding of the elevator distracted her from her paranoid delusions. Turning around, she saw it disgorging the couple who lived across the hall from her. Relieved at their timely arrival, which broke the spell of fear that had frozen her, she dashed into the empty cubicle and stabbed the button to go down. Arriving at the lobby, she saw the yellow cab already sitting at the curb. She clambered in.

"Where to, ma'am?" asked the driver.

"Um . . ." For a moment her mind went blank. Where did she want to go? The places she knew were also frequented by Tom and Becky, a pair she definitely didn't want to run into. "Do you know of any bars nearby with good music and a dance floor?"

"Sure do. What do you prefer, country, dance, or jazz?"

Jazz and its usual blues might prove too depressing for her current state of mind. Dance music, while her usual fave, was a little too hyper still for her mood. "Country, please." She leaned back against the seat as the taxi sped away from the curb.

A partial smile tilted her lips as she thought of hooking up with a cowboy. It made her think of that song that said to ride a cowboy and save a horse. She didn't think she was ready for anything that intimate yet, but some good old-fashioned attraction to the opposite sex, and some slow dancing plastered against a tall, jean-clad hunk, would probably go a long way toward soothing her tender heart.

Arriving at the bar, which proved a little farther

than expected at the town's limits, she paid the driver and got out. The place didn't look like much and seemed a little too stereotypical with its weather-beaten wooden façade and flashing neon sign comprised of red cowboy boots. The parking lot appeared packed with pickup trucks and SUVs, with the occasional car thrown in, a true cowboy haven that almost made her question her choice. However, the beat of the music, catchy and toe tapping, filled the air outside. Loud as it seemed out here, it would probably prove thunderous indoors. Perfect. She wasn't ready to socialize yet, not until she got a drink or two in her. Despite her lone state and the corny setting, she found herself drumming her foot to the rhythm, excitement threading through her. Taking a deep breath, she ignored the trepidation that tried to chip away at her courage. *I can do this.*

Bailey walked in. A wave of noise, heat, and scents washed over her. *Too much!* She almost ran back out.

Standing for a moment, breathing evenly, she took in the scene of chaos. Voices battled for supremacy with the music, which consisted of a lot of guitar and crooning. The crowd seemed evenly split for the most part, with both sides of the sexes represented from what looked like barely legal to wizened in the last century. And everywhere she looked, jeans, plaid, and boots were the agreed-upon dress code, the only variation occurring in the color and newness of said clothing. She fit right in with her ensemble.

The door behind her opened, and she knew she couldn't stand there like a ninny forever. Forcing her feet into motion, she weaved her way through the crowd, making her way to the bar, not as simple as it sounded with the press of bodies. However, she needed a boost of liquid courage.

A jostle from behind saw her pushed into someone seated on a stool, a man obviously descended from boulders considering how hard and unyielding his body proved.

Her hands flailed out to steady her, one landing on a thickly muscled thigh, the other caught by a warm and firm grip. Another hand, belonging to the man she'd bumped into, settled on her waist. A tingling awareness of his touch made her suck in a breath. Raising her eyes, she opened her mouth to say sorry but ended up gaping instead.

Was Lady Luck or fate listening when I said I wanted to meet a handsome cowboy?

Deep blue eyes framed in dark lashes perused her, at odds with the light-colored brows and blond hair that crowned his head. A slow, sexy smile that shot heat through her curved his sensual lips. He leaned closer, almost enough she could have tasted him, and her tummy tightened at the musky scent of him, a mixture of cologne and *man.*

He spoke loud enough for her to hear him above the music. "Well, hello there, darling. Crowd's a little rowdy tonight for a little thing like you." He pulled back to peer at her.

Little? He'd obviously not gotten a good look at her. Tongue-tied for a second, Bailey could only nod her head as embarrassment stained her cheeks. "S-Sorry about that. It's kind of hard to get around in here."

She didn't speak as loudly as she should have, and she doubted he could hear her over the music, but he nodded as if he did. He leaned over until his lips hovered just over her ear, his warm breath in the shell of it making her bite back a sigh. "That it is. Why don't you sit here out of harm's way?"

Before she could protest, he'd slid from the barstool and plucked her up effortlessly to seat her in his place. His casual strength caught her attention. While not a really huge girl, Bailey owned a few extra pounds on her hips, butt, boobs, and thighs, giving her a nice cushion—she wasn't exactly a dainty flower.

The stranger leaned into her again, his lips this time actually brushing her ear, sending shivers down her spine.

"What are you drinking?" he asked before signaling the bartender.

"Oh, I couldn't." Mum always told her not to accept drinks unless she wanted a man to get the impression she intended to put out. Although, given how her heart raced, and the heat pooled her cleft, perhaps this was one time she could test that theory.

"I insist," he murmured, his voice low and

caressing. Bailey swallowed and clenched her legs together as her whole body reacted to his sensual promise.

The nameless cowboy, dressed in a worn plaid shirt and even more broken-in jeans that hugged his lean hips, held up two fingers. A moment later two beers landed in front of them, condensation rolling down their brown glass sides.

"Thanks," she muttered, dropping her eyes.

"My pleasure. Come here often?"

"My first time actually." She blushed as she realized how that sounded.

A chuckle escaped him and brushed her skin almost like a caress. "So you live around here?"

"Downtown."

"You meeting somebody?"

She heard the question in his voice—*Do you have boyfriend?* She smiled and shook her head. "Nope. Trying to be brave and make some friends." The moment she said it, she wanted to slap herself. How corny and desperate did that sound?

He, however, smiled at her, not an ounce of pity in his gaze but lots of sensual interest. "Well, you've met one. My name's Gavin, by the way."

Before she could reply and give her own name, a second body closed in on her other side. Bailey gulped because the new stranger, glaring at her blond cowboy, appeared just as hunky. Dark-haired, he sported a tanned complexion that proved a striking combination with his dark eyes. Dressed in a white T-shirt and jeans, he appeared as hard and muscled as Gavin. Sandwiched between them, Bailey fought an urge to swoon—and touch.

As if sensing her racing heart and sweaty palms, the stranger swiveled to meet her gaze with intent black. Bailey blushed under the newcomer's perusal and dragged her gaze away to stare at the top of the scarred bar.

"I now see what has you distracted," the dark-haired hunk stated, his gravelly tone low but loud enough for her to hear. "But your plans for seduction will have to wait. What we're seeking isn't here."

"I wouldn't be so sure of that," said Gavin, tossing her a smile that heightened the color in her cheeks.

"Cute as she is," the dark one replied, grabbing her attention, "you'll have to explore your interest later. We have a job to do."

Confused at the undercurrent that passed between the two men, Bailey turned her head to see her blond cowboy now sporting a grimace.

"Sorry, darling. I'm afraid my friend here is being most adamant about reminding me I have some business to take care of. I don't suppose you'd give me your number so I can call you?"

Ha, like he'd call her. He must have seen the doubt in her eyes because he smiled at her.

"I understand your caution. We are, after all, almost strangers, but I would like to change that.

Since you just arrived at the bar, I'm hoping you'll hang around for a bit. I shouldn't be gone more than an hour or two. If you stay, will you save a dance for me?"

Bailey wordlessly nodded then blushed furiously as he swept in close and brushed his lips against her cheek. A brief, yet scorching contact that made her heart pump double time.

"Later, darling."

It was with bemusement that Bailey watched her fair-haired hunk and his darker companion, who tossed her an enigmatic look over his shoulder, stride through the crowd to the outer doors and leave. She couldn't help watching the door for a moment, almost wishing they'd turn around and come right back—for her.

Foolishness, of course, but definitely fantasy worthy. Talk about heart-stoppingly gorgeous— both of them. She didn't for a minute believe Gavin would remember her once he finished whatever business called him so late, but it stroked her ego to know she'd even caught his interest in the first place.

Catching herself staring toward the entrance— still apparently hoping he would come back sooner than he expected—she sighed as she turned back to the bar and her waiting beer. It hadn't taken long for someone in the crowd to slip into the empty spot Gavin had just vacated. Unlike her blond cowboy, though, the new fellow didn't inspire lusty thoughts of any kind. Actually, with his bright, almost feverish eyes and his wide smile that showed too many teeth, her new neighbor made her stomach tighten unpleasantly. Grasping her beer, she slid off the stool and moved away, losing herself in the crowd.

A sip of the pungent brew and she grimaced. Nasty stuff. Nasty and yet she took another sip, and another, soon finding dizzy, a combination of the booze heat and music going right to her head. She put down the brown bottle and weaved her way to the bathroom, her stomach roiling and her sight blurring.

What on earth? She didn't have a high tolerance for booze, but still, she hadn't even finished one drink, which made her current state seem odd. Bailey staggered and hit the wall before the bathroom. She blinked her eyes, but each time she closed her lids, it became harder to open them back up. A numbing languor spread through her body.

I've been drugged!

The mental admission didn't stop her knees from buckling, but before she could hit the floor, hands grasped her and held her upright. Had her sexy cowboy returned?

A whiff of rancid sweat made her cringe, and a voice in her head howled—*Run!* A futile command, given her body wouldn't function. She also never got a chance to see who'd caught her because she blinked one last time and slipped into darkness.

* * * *

Gavin didn't welcome Wyatt's interruption, and neither did his wolf. He especially didn't like the interest in his pack brother's eyes as he looked upon the human female who'd literally bumped into him.

Something about the dark-haired, shy creature drew him—and made him harder than a rod of steel. Damn, he didn't remember the last time, if any, the simple presence of a female affected him so.

When he took his leave, with a promise to return later, he meant it, especially after his brief taste of her skin and scent. Even though the woman was obviously not pack, she called to him. Only a stupid wolf, or one determined to limit himself by frolicking only with his kind, would ignore her appeal. In the Lycan world, the males outnumber the females in large numbers. And the she-wolves they had weren't for casual fucking. If a Lycan maid caught a male's eye, then he either mated with her or went without. A male wolf also had to accept his place as only one of several mates.

Lycan females were expected to take on at least two men, sometimes more. It was a pack law, a law the council leader, Nathan, and his mate, Dana, were trying to change. But politics moved slowly, even with Lycans. So far, Nathan had succeeded in at least allowing the females to choose their own husbands, unlike the previous archaic way of having a father select for the wrong reasons or, in rarer cases, the claiming, often by force, of an unmated female. But the low number of females made limiting matings to one of each sex still a futile dream.

So, how did this tie in to the delectable human he'd met? No matter the law, the fact remained that finding a mate within his own species was almost impossible and keeping her to himself even less likely. Gavin also knew not all males found their mate in their lifetime, and not all mates were Lycan.

Could the little darling be the one destined as his? Her humanity would prevent conception between them, but at the same time, her lack of Lycan gene meant he could keep her to himself.

However, he was getting ahead of himself. Intriguing as he found the curly-haired cutie, it didn't mean she was *the one*. Only time, a more thorough taste, and fate would tell.

"So who was the curvy mouthful?" Wyatt asked as they escaped the noise and crowd in the bar.

Gavin stifled a growl as his possessive side woke. "I don't know. You interrupted me before we even got past the hellos."

"Well excuse me for thinking we had a job to do here."

"You don't need to remind me of my task." Wyatt arched a brow in reply, and Gavin chuckled wryly. "Okay, maybe I needed a little nudge. But damn me, there was something about her."

"Something enticing," Wyatt added.

His friend's answer stunned him. "You felt it

too?"

His pack brother nodded. "She's not wolf, but my damned beast was whining at me to sniff her and then lick her all over."

Gavin's own beast paced in his mind, and a low growl of jealousy almost forced its way past his control. He couldn't help himself from saying, though, "I saw her first. So hands off."

"Why? Afraid she'd prefer my mug to yours?"

"Not really because we both know I'm nicer."

"Says you. Besides, who says we have to fight over her? My father always did say sharing was the best plan."

Gavin groaned. "We are not going to talk about your father right now. I still haven't recovered from the sex talk he gave me at eleven. Some things a boy shouldn't know."

"Hey, he thought he was doing you a favor what with your dad gone and all," Wyatt replied defensively.

Gavin slapped Wyatt on the back. "I know, which is why I've kept you alive, you annoying dick." And stepbrother. Gavin's mother was mated with three men, of which Wyatt's father was one. After Gavin's father died in a logging accident, it seemed natural for Kevin, Wyatt's dad, and also a widower, to take him under his wing.

A snort sounded as Wyatt opened the truck door. "Oh please. We both know the reason you became my friend is because you know I'd kick your ass in a second."

"Ha."

Their bantering, a familiar routine held over from their youth, continued on as they traveled to the next bar in search of rogues.

Gavin actually did have business to take care of, council business. The Lycan packs answered to the council, who set the laws and enforced them. Gavin and his group of pack brothers were one of their sets of enforcers. Chosen because of their strength and abilities to hunt—as well as kill—they traveled at the council's behest, taking care of problems before the humans took note.

In this case, they hunted rogues, defined as wolves who no longer belonged to a pack and who behaved without any regard for the laws and the consequences of their actions. In the last few years, they'd seen an upsurge in rogue incidents, a surge in males abandoning the packs for a lawless life, or disappearing entirely leaving homes and families behind.

In a twist, it turned out their own Lycan council was at fault. Or at least one member was. Was being the key given he was executed for dereliction of duty for giving some of their own kind to the vampires. Yes vampires, a species thought to be a myth.

Wrong, at least according to Nathan, the new head of council. According to their esteemed leader, Nathan's own supposedly dead father was the one luring folks away from the pack to give to the blood suckers. Apparently, Roderick was not only the force behind the disappearances, he was now half Lycan, half vampire.

Personally, Gavin had to wonder if their leader, Nathan, had gone off the deep end because, seriously, vampires? Sure, werewolves existed, but bloodsuckers who could also control minds? That really stretched things.

Gavin's theory was Nathan suffered from guilt because he had to dispose of his father when he went mentally unstable and began harming his pack instead of protecting it. This guilt made Nathan see his father as some kind of ultimate evil behind the ever-increasing rogue problems.

Regardless of their pack leader's mental state, Gavin couldn't deny rogues were bad for all Lycans, no matter who stood behind ordering them or, as Nathan claimed, mentally commanding them.

As to their current assignment, they'd received reports of rogues sighted in the area, enough of them to cause concern, even though this sector didn't currently have an active pack. They'd arrived a week ago, and while they'd caught vague traces of wolf in the area, they'd yet to encounter any.

Of more concern were the disappearances of the human women within a hundred-mile radius who kept reappearing dead, their bodies raped, beaten, and clawed as if by wild animals. The newspaper had barely touched on the murderous rampage, probably because, up until a few weeks ago, the missing women were ladies of the night, aka prostitutes, who probably ranked low on the crime-solving radar. As far as the public knew, the first kidnapping had occurred about two weeks ago, and the police, for some reason, weren't correcting the misconception.

It made him think of the little darling from the bar. Alone, she appeared a tempting target, but he couldn't allow his newfound protective instinct toward a veritable stranger deter him from his mission. The bar he'd just left appeared clean, not a scent of wolf anywhere to be found. And, with his kiss, he'd left his mark on her, warning others off—hopefully.

If Gavin intended to smear his scent more thoroughly on her—while enjoying himself immensely—then he'd have to do his duty first. So off he went with Wyatt, barhopping in the hopes of finding a rogue trail. His other pack brothers, Jaxon and Parker, were doing the same. Just another dull day of searching, where they'd later meet back at the cabins they'd rented and compare notes.

A few hours later, longer than Gavin expected, they ended up back at the country bar. "What a waste of time," Gavin complained. "I swear it's like the bastards know we're coming and scatter. That last place, I thought I had one. I still don't understand how they're hiding their tracks so well."

"I'll agree it's frustrating," Wyatt replied in a low tone. "But we've got to keep looking. If we haven't found anything concrete by the end of the week, we'll try in the next town over."

Wyatt's suggestion didn't entirely please Gavin. Leaving town meant leaving the dark-haired cutie he'd just met, the one he hoped to see again— tonight.

Gavin pretended nonchalance as he entered the still-rocking place, but Wyatt thumped him on the back and laughed.

"Careful or you're going to scare her away with that hungry look of yours."

Chagrined that his control had slipped enough to make his desires evident on his face, Gavin schooled his features as he scanned the place. He couldn't locate his little darling's scent, that sweet blend of honey shampoo and baby powder deodorant. Too many odors crowded his senses, making sifting them difficult. He moved toward the bar itself, halting at the stool where she'd perched before. Too many bodies had since occupied it for him to scent her. Turning to regard the crowd it didn't take long for his excitement to slump. She'd left.

It made no sense for him to feel so disappointed. He'd just met her, a simple human girl. Yet, despite the brevity of their meeting, and her human status, he couldn't stop himself from wondering how he could find her again.

A sharp poke in his side snapped him from his thoughts, and he turned to see a somber-looking Wyatt gesturing at him to follow.

"What's up?"

Wyatt didn't bother answering as Gavin followed him to the corridor that led to the bathrooms. "Need me to watch your back while you pee?" Gavin joked.

"Smell."

Gavin inhaled. He sifted the myriad scents, the perfumes, and sweat, and . . . found a faint trace of his mystery woman. And wolf. Make that unknown wolves. A ball of dread made his stomach tighten as he followed the scent trail—wolf, wolf, and honey shampoo.

Stuck to his heels, Wyatt kept up with him as Gavin went down the hall to the emergency exit and out into the back of the place. Once outside, Gavin turned left, and then right, breathing deep each time, before taking off at a jog toward the edge of the woods, where he finally lost the trail.

"We missed them," Wyatt announced grimly. "They must have arrived after we left."

"No shit, Sherlock. But the better question is, why did they take my mystery lady with them?"

Wyatt's face scrunched into a grimace. "Shit, I thought the scent seemed familiar. Fuck, you don't think they're going to—"

"Kill her like they did the others?" Cold fingers of fear squeezed his heart. "Not if we find her first. According to reports, the other women had been kept alive anywhere from a week to a month. We'll need to move fast."

"Gee, like we've been sitting on our hands this

entire time. We still don't have any more clues than before."

Gavin knelt at the edge of the brush bordering the parking lot and pulled from the weeds a small black wallet with a wrist strap. Opening it, he ignored the cash and pulled out credit cards and a bank card, all with the name of Bailey Donovan. He found tucked into a pocket a picture of his woman with an older couple who resembled her. "Well at least we know who she is."

"We do?"

Gavin held up his find. "Come on. Let's go check her place out and see if we find any clues."

Whipping his cell phone out as Wyatt maneuvered their truck through the darkened streets, Gavin called Parker and Jaxon.

Jaxon answered. "Yo, mighty leader. I was just about to head back to the cabin. Want me to grab a few pizzas?"

"Change of plans. I need you to meet me at . . ." He read the address off of Bailey's ID card.

"What's up, boss?"

"There's been another rogue abduction. Check out the outside while Wyatt and I do a search of her apartment."

Hanging up, Gavin drummed his fingers on the armrest. Anger that he'd left her fueled his ire. If only he'd stayed, listened to his inner desire to get to know her better, he might have prevented her abduction.

"It's not your fault," Wyatt said softly.

"If I'd just stuck around a little longer, I would have caught them before they took her."

"Or scared them off to snatch someone else."

Gavin's lips drew tight before he blurted out the words that came to mind: *But I don't give a damn about someone else.* It galled him that he'd come so close to finally spotting the rogues. It galled him even more that he hadn't given in to temptation and stayed with Bailey, his shy temptress, a little longer. And it killed him to know they'd taken her, were probably hurting her at this very moment, and there wasn't a damned thing he could do about it. Yet.

Arriving at her place, a high-rise building made of gray cement and festooned with brown rusted balconies, they parked around the corner before hiking back. They vetoed the front entrance, which was well lighted and locked. As they slid around to the back, the scent of wolf hit them. With his jaw tight, Gavin followed the smell right up to a service door and yanked on the handle. It gave easily, the reason being someone had taped the latch so it wouldn't trip.

Gavin followed the trail of the rogues, two by his count, and not the ones from the bar, up the stairs, stopping at the seventh floor, where the scent led out into the hall. Castigating himself even further for having left Bailey, a woman they'd obviously hunted beforehand, he ghosted through the silent corridor, wondering if the perpetrators remained inside.

The door to her apartment opened at his touch, already unlocked. Shutting the door behind Wyatt, Gavin blew out a breath.

"They're not here."

Not in person at any rate, but they'd left the signs of their visit behind. The place had been tossed and destroyed. Cushions with the stuffing ripped out littered the floor. Detritus, from glass to paper to what looked like food, decorated the place, as if the rogues had gone on a destructive spree.

How come the cops weren't called?

He knew, though. Humans no longer protected their own. They didn't want to get involved in the problems of others.

Wading through the mess, Gavin fought an urge to punch something, to cause some destruction of his own.

"They were looking for something," Wyatt said from behind him.

"How can you tell from this mess?" Gavin snorted, gesturing with an outward flung hand.

"Because they only dumped the two drawers of her desk and left the rest intact. See?"

Gavin peered over and saw what Wyatt meant. He strode over and knelt to sift through the two piles on the floor.

"Insurance papers, medical receipts, income tax papers, bills." He noted a pair of death certificates for Mary Jean and Joseph Donovan, dated only a year ago. A twinge in Gavin's heart made him recognize sorrow for the woman he still barely knew, one who'd lost both her parents in one fell swoop.

"See a pattern yet?" Wyatt asked.

"It's all her personal shit. So what? Maybe they got interrupted, or whoever nabbed her called them to tell them to ditch the place."

"Stop looking at the simple and obvious. Use your brain for something other than filler for your skull. What's missing?"

A growl almost left his mouth at his beta's goading. But Wyatt wouldn't provoke him without reason. Gavin's brows drew together as he looked at all the papers. He riffled through them some more and located Bailey's father's birth certificate and his driver's license, lots of things for Joseph, but other than the death certificate, nothing identifying for Mary Jean. "The mother's stuff is missing."

"Yes, as is Bailey's birth certificate, I'll bet," Wyatt added.

"So you don't think she was a random choice? They chose her because of her mother?"

"It's a possibility."

"Why would murderous, raping bastards care?" Gavin almost yelled as he stood, his impotence fueling his anger.

Wyatt shrugged. "I guess it's something we'll have to find out."

"Let's get out of here. We're not going to find her trail sifting through this."

Exiting as surreptitiously as they had arrived, they met up with Jaxon and Parker at the truck.

"Find anything?" Gavin asked without greeting.

Jaxon took a step back and held up his hands. "Whoa, what's got your boxers in a bunch? Jeez, you'd think they stole your mother the way you're frowning."

"He met the girl at the bar who was taken. Took quite a shine to her too."

"I wasn't the only one who noticed she was something special," Gavin growled.

"Damn, boss. That sucks. Wish we had better news then. Whoever it was cased the joint. One hung out in the alleyway bordering the place and the parking lot behind it. Another fellow was watching across the street. Unfortunately, they had wheels, so once they hightailed it, I lost their trail."

"Great, another dead end." Gavin raked his fingers through his hair and blew out a tired sigh.

"We need to get back to the cabin and get some sleep."

"I can't. She's out there somewhere with those animals."

"And you're not going to do her any good if you're exhausted and not thinking straight. We'll hit this again with a fresh outlook tomorrow night."

It galled Gavin that Wyatt spoke the truth. Fatigue did pull at him, but so did fear that every moment he wasn't searching, they were hurting Bailey, the lady with the shy smile and warm eyes.

However, getting himself murdered or making stupid mistakes would hurt her even more, so even though it just about killed him to call off the hunt for the night, he did.

Back at the cabin, sleep eluded him, abetted by his restless wolf, who paced in his mind as if demanding why they weren't out in the woods hunting the rogues down, tracking the woman who intrigued them. He would, as soon he knew where to start to looking.

Hold on, Bailey. I will find you.

Chapter Two

Waking up with a pounding head didn't bode well, but regaining consciousness to realize she hung, naked and manacled, spread-eagle, totally beat any hangover. And scared the bejesus out of Bailey.

Everything in her body hurt. Pinpointing the origin of her pain proved elusive, though. Even her teeth and hair ached. It made her scared to open her eyes.

Was I involved in an accident?

She didn't even own a car, let alone recall getting into one. The last thing she did remember was the bar and that handsome cowboy who'd left her sipping on her drink as she wandered around, getting in the mood to dance, then . . . nothing.

A dark figure with glowing eyes . . .

The feeble image slipped away. A hazy fog clouded her memories, and fear joined the agony of her body. *Someone slipped me a Mickey.* All the warnings she'd heard over the years, mostly paranoid speeches from her mum, ran through her mind. And yet, she'd guarded her drink, or so she thought, receiving it directly from the bartender and not leaving it unattended.

Except when I turned to watch Gavin leave.

She recalled the leering fellow who'd taken Gavin's place at the bar. In that moment of inattention, had he drugged her? Not that the who mattered. Regardless of who'd taken her, she still found herself strung up in an untenable situation.

A catalog of her body didn't point to any one injury, more like an all-over pain that made her throb. Even her jaw ached, as if she'd clenched her teeth all night. *Or screamed like a madwoman* . . . Her mind veered away from that train of thought to something less likely to give her hysterics, if that was even possible in this situation.

How long have I been here?

Without a window, or anything else to provide a time frame, she could have hung there minutes or days.

The dark one returned, his cackling laughter joining my screams as I . . .

Again, the weak memory slipped from her grasp. Yet, how could such a thing be real? As quickly as her mind phrased the question, it forgot.

Attempting to focus on something concrete, she strained to hear something, anything. Hope, in the form of police sirens, would have been nice.

The faint sound of moans, scattered with nonsensical gibbering, floated through the bars on the door of her prison. Bailey chewed her lip, wondering what kind of torture could reduce someone to that kind of dejection and fear. What did it take to strip someone's humanity?

A scraping at the door brought her head up, and she stared intently as it swung open. At the first glimpse of red eyes, her memories came rushing back in a roar, and even before he touched her, she began to scream then thrash as he did things to her, horrible things that filled her with pain. His torture tore wails of terror from her, shrill screams that went on and on until she grew hoarse, an ongoing nightmare that made her lose track of time. Not that she remembered the moments of agony, for each time he left, he took the memories of his time with her away, leaving her to agonize afresh each time she woke, slowly losing her humanity—and her mind.

* * * *

Wyatt watched as Gavin punched yet another tree in frustration. For days now, they'd searched for signs of the rogues, but since the abduction of the girl, they'd disappeared. This lack of clue, or even faint trail to them, was driving Gavin slowly insane.

And over a human chit. Admittedly, Bailey appeared cute with her rounded frame and shy smile. However, Wyatt didn't obsess over the fact she'd gotten taken. Okay, not true, it bugged the hell out of him, but he hadn't taken it as personally as Gavin.

"Where the hell did they take her?" Gavin growled for the umpteenth time.

"The rogues ain't around here, if you ask me," Jaxon said. "We'd have caught a trace of them by now."

"I think it's time we widened our search circle," Parker interjected in his deep rumble.

"Easier said than done," Wyatt replied. "Which direction do you think we should choose? They could be anywhere. All the abductions occurred in this area and were all recovered here as well."

"Exactly." Gavin sat up straight, his eyes lighting up even with the fatigue clouding them. "Parker has a point. These rogues are wily. Does it seem likely they'd hunt and dump on their home turf?"

"You're probably right, but again, where do we take our search next?"

"Food."

"How many times a day do you have to be fed, Jaxon? Christ, we ate like an hour ago," Gavin grumbled as the youngest of their group threw their discussion off course.

"No, I mean, even rogues need food. So why the heck are we wasting our time searching every goddamned bar, woods, motel, hotel, you name it in this stupid town when we could just be hitting grocery stores? They have to eat, don't they?"

The logic of it, so simple and neat, made Wyatt want to smack himself in the head. He smacked Jaxon instead, and at his friend's disgruntled look, a chuckle erupted from Wyatt's lips. "I don't believe it, but I do believe our little puppy here has a point. How many grocery stores can there be?"

"What if they're shopping at a 7-Eleven?" Parker

asked.

"If you're feeding a group of wolves, you're going to need lots of red meat. Only a market will carry that," Wyatt explained.

"Good thinking, Jaxon. Wyatt!" Gavin barked. "Pull up the directions to all the grocery stores in a two-hour radius from here. It's time to go shopping."

It took them fourteen stores and a day and a half, but they finally caught a scent. After that, given the small size of the town, it became only a matter of hours before they narrowed the possible rogue hideout to a dozen or so places.

Noses to the ground, quite literally, they proceeded to winnow that number down.

A day later, they hit the jackpot.

Chapter Three

Blinking her eyes at the white ceiling, Bailey took a moment to enjoy the fact that her body no longer hurt. The screaming pain, the throbbing of her joints, the ache of her muscles all appeared gone.

I've died.

On the heels of that thought, she frowned. What on earth made her think any of those things? Not recalling any injury done to her person, it seemed foolish to wake up feeling relief she no longer hurt. *Did I have a bad dream?*

It seemed the only likely explanation. However . . . that didn't explain the unfamiliar expanse over her head.

How had she arrived here? Where was here?

Bailey closed her eyes as she cast her recollection backward. A shiver of unease shook her body as, for a moment, in her mind's eye, she glimpsed glowing eyes, a fanciful imagery probably left over from whatever dream she'd experienced that left her thinking she'd gotten injured.

A murky haze seemed to hover over her recollections, the sense of time passed, and yet, the last thing she recalled, she hung out in a Western bar, surrounded by noise and people. *And now I'm in a strange bed? Good God, did I get drunk and screw some stranger?*

Hopefully, if she had completely thrown caution to the wind, she'd done so with the handsome cowboy. But as the fuzzy cloud of sleep left her mind, more memories crowded in. She recalled becoming dizzy then falling, only to have someone catch her, someone who leered and smelled awful. Her memories after that became fractured with scattered recollections of being carried—*pain, white-hot agony joined by gravelly laughter as she hung suspended, trapped*—and dumped on this bed, her kidnappers arguing about whether to use restraints or not.

Panic made her move. Thrashing her arms and legs, she discovered nothing fettered her, although she noticed as she sat up for a better look at her surroundings that she didn't wear any clothes. Dread made her heart stutter as immediately thoughts of rape raced through her mind, and she ran her hands over her body, looking for signs of abuse. Nothing came to light, but still her tension remained taut, the sense of injury done to her person strong. Yet, her thighs appeared dry and clean, her body whole and unblemished. Perhaps she'd woken before her abductors achieved their objective? She couldn't help shuddering as she remembered the news on the girl who'd disappeared. *Have I just become the next victim?* Not if she could help it.

I need to get out of here. But exactly where was here? A clue of any kind seemed in order, and she peered about.

Despite the white ceiling, the rest of the room appeared shabby and unkempt. The wallpaper, patterned in flowers, peeled in places. On a second glance, she noted spiderwebs on the ceiling and the hairline cracks running through it. Getting up from the bed, a raunchy mattress covered in rust-colored stains—which her mind preferred not to dwell on— her feet touched a bare wooden floor, the varnish lost amidst the scratches of age.

All in all, things didn't look good. *Actually, it's pretty bloody scary.* A scream wound its way up her chest, caught in her constricted throat. She held on to that outward expression of fear because it seemed unlikely, given her surroundings, that someone would come to her rescue if she screamed. More than likely any kind of sound would instead bring . . .

Danger. Run.

Her inner voice, the one that had guided her for most of her life, spoke up, stronger than she ever recalled. Heeding the warning, Bailey whirled and searched for escape. It took her only a second to discard the closed door because she knew that would only lead into the arms of her captor. Or worse.

A single window was set in the wall, and a brief glance out showed nothing but darkness. A frantic tug at the sash yielded nothing but frustration. Thwarted, she slammed her hands against the wooden sash, noticing only too late the ragged nails holding it shut. The edge of one caught at her skin, tearing it, and blood flowed from the wound. The crimson trail threatened to drip, so she absently stuck her wounded digit in her mouth, tasting the metallic fluid and strangely enjoying it. She sucked at the blood, a low growl escaping her when the flow stopped. Appalled at her actions—and desire for more—she pulled her hand from her mouth and stared at it. Incomprehension flooded her as she gazed at the unblemished skin.

But I saw the cut there. I know I did. I tasted the blood. She'd healed spontaneously.

Not understanding what this meant, and frightened by it, she turned to the door, the only other exit from the room and her only choice, like it or not.

On bare feet, she approached it, her nerves taut and her breathing coming shallowly. She placed her hand on the tarnished knob and turned it.

It swiveled.

Astonishment made her let go. Why had they left it unlocked? Was it a trick? *Perhaps I jumped to conclusions and I haven't been abducted at all.*

Holding her breath for a moment, Bailey listened, her ears straining for a sign someone waited on the other side, any kind of noise to show she wasn't alone. Nothing came back to her, other than the faint creaking of an old house settling with age. She grasped the knob again and turned it. This time she didn't release it when the latch clicked and the door crept open. Pulling it toward her, certain at any moment the bogeyman would jump out and yell, *"Boo,"* she couldn't believe her luck, didn't trust it.

Nothing lurked out in the hall. On tiptoe, she snuck down the corridor, wincing at the faint creak as the floor underfoot gave under her weight. Pausing at the head of the stairs, where the faint glow of a light below illuminated the worn treads, she finally heard some noise, more like a whimper. She peeked down the stairs and then back up the hall, where another plaintive cry sounded.

Bailey chewed her lip as indecision gripped her. *Do I go for help or try to help?* That moment cost her. The door from whence the crying came opened, and a man exited, still buttoning up his pants. Raising his head, he froze when he saw her. Not reassuring given his appearance; unshaven, his hair shaggy and wild. His leering smile sent chills down her spine and dispelled any last illusion she still harbored that she wasn't in danger.

"Well, look at what we've got here. You're an eager little slut, aren't you? Coming to find me for your turn, were you?" The ruffian grabbed at his crotch and thrust it in her direction.

Disgust made her stomach roil. Shaking her head, Bailey kept her eyes trained on the man as her foot slipped back, looking for purchase on the first step.

"Where do you think you're going, my chubby slut? The master brought you here for our use. He told us to plow that belly of yours good and hard. I gotta say I've been waiting for this moment." He licked his lips, and bile coated the back of her mouth, making her eyes water. "He kept you down there for a while. Screaming and begging. I'll bet you he's got you worked in real good now. Are you gonna scream nice and loud for me too when I take you?"

What was he talking about? The words of the miscreant spun in her mind but made no sense. He talked as if Bailey were the victim of torture and possibly even rape, and yet, she bore no signs of either.

Shaking her head wildly in denial, she slid her other foot to join the first, landing half on the step. Not losing her fixed stare at the approaching brute, she made her way down the stairs backward. *He's just trying to freak me out.* He probably thrived on his victim's fear. *And he's succeeding. I am so scared right now.* But she daren't let herself falter, not with the deadly promise in his flat eyes.

A creak from below caught her attention, and she darted a look down.

Oh no. Another man, this one familiar because she remembered him from the bar, had his foot on the first step. He leered up at her.

A shadow fell over her as the first thug hit the top of the stairs. "So who's going to be first, me or Leroy here? Or maybe you'd like us both at the same time?"

A low wail built up in her chest but couldn't escape, not through a throat clenched tight in fear. Caught between the two of them, she shook. She couldn't let them touch her. Couldn't let them do what she saw in their eyes and menacing smiles.

I'd rather die.

When the guy below her got close enough, she gathered herself and launched her body at him. She caught him off guard and hit him, hard enough that she threw him off balance. Arms windmilling, he teetered then fell.

Unfortunately, given her momentum, she plummeted with him.

Bailey felt every solid step she hit, bruises blossoming in the jolting wake, followed by pain. She lucked out on a soft landing, though, as she ended up on top of a groaning Leroy, who hadn't fared as well, it seemed.

Not wasting time, she scrambled to her feet, the sound of feet pounding down the stairs too close for comfort. Lucky for her, the front door opened on the first pull, and she dashed out into darkness.

A howl erupted behind her, an inhuman sound that made her mind stray to a dark corner better left untouched.

Not thinking, not bothering to pause and take her bearings, she leapt off the porch and ran.

She sprinted, arms pumping, chest heaving, her breathing coming in whimpering pants while her blood surged through her body. Floating like the wind, her bare feet seemed to barely touch the ground and didn't register the debris in her path. She tore through the trees and bramble with no clear destination in mind other than escape. She ran as if her life depended on it because she knew that if she didn't, she would die, felt that with a certainty in the marrow of her bones and a chilling fear that made her gulp air in harsh sobs.

Behind her, the crackling of fallen leaves and steady thumps signaled pursuit, but it was the baying, the exultant voices of the predators chasing her, raised in a chorus, that made her skin pimple. Not the barking of dogs, although they would have proven dangerous on their own. The eerie howling reminded her of . . .

Wolves? Seriously? A hysterical giggle got caught in her throat at the thought she might have escaped death at human hands, only to possibly find it in the jaws of an animal. But only if they caught her.

It surprised her that she'd found the energy to flee. After all, she'd been drugged and fallen down a flight of stairs. She would have expected to feel weak. Instead, she discovered strength, a stamina unlike any she'd ever known. Stranger, she didn't feel any pain from her surely bruised body. Then again, she'd heard adrenaline could make a person do just about anything. Throw in a need for survival, and she'd probably leap buildings, too, if they ended up in her path.

Movement out of the corner of her eye caught

her attention. She turned her head sideways and stumbled as the yellow glowing eyes, tinged in red, of a predator met hers. As if her attention were a signal, it veered and leapt at her.

A scream escaped her as the heavy body hit her in the side, taking her to the ground. The impact made her grunt, and her breath left her in a whoosh. Fingers scrabbling at the dirt, limbs thrashing, she only managed to turn herself until she lay on her back. The wolf unfortunately followed, his heavy body astride hers.

Instinct made her push her hands up to grasp at the underside of the creature's jaws as it snapped at her.

Foiled, it growled, low and menacing. Bailey whimpered in fear, struggling against the heavy body and fighting to keep its slavering jaws away.

Hysteria made her eyes water, and she keened, a forlorn sound that she scarcely recognized as coming from her. She didn't know how long she could keep the beast at bay and wondered why she bothered. Did she seriously think she could outwrestle a wolf?

The thought no sooner crossed her mind than the body atop hers went tumbling sideways as something hit it. Bailey lay there panting for a moment, incomprehension not allowing her to register what she saw at first.

Eyes adjusted to the darkness to a certain extent, she peered in disbelief. A second wolf, or a huge dog, had joined the fray, but instead of aiding the first beast, the new wild canine snapped at it. Even more peculiar, her furry rescuer's eyes shone a vivid green. The black-haired beast caught her gaze and tossed its head at her, as if signaling her away.

Impossible, and surely a product of her wishful mind, but Bailey obeyed anyway, scrambling to her feet and taking off again. The sounds of primitive battle receded as she resumed her race through the forest. However, she hadn't left danger behind. The number of baying voices seemed to treble, and the wetness of her fearful tears almost made her blind.

The sound of pursuit, crackling leaves and snapping branches, approached once again, and she whimpered.

She'd gotten lucky once. She doubted she'd get lucky again.

Head craned backward, her eyes darted about, she frantically sought the approaching menace. Distracted, she ended up missing the solid trunk in front of her, but she felt it as she hit it full on and bounced back. Not a tree, she belatedly realized, but scorching, smooth skin.

A shriek escaped her as hands grasped her before she fell. *Caught!* Her strident wail almost sounded like a howl.

"Shh, darling. It's okay now. I've got you."

The soothing words didn't penetrate her panic, and she thrashed against her captor. He tightened his arms around her, plastering her to his chest, murmuring softly, until finally, with a deep sob, she stopped fighting, and she realized who held her.

A familiar musky scent surrounded her, one she clearly remembered even though she'd only briefly encountered it once before. "G-Gavin?" she hiccupped.

"Yes, darling. It's me. I've been looking for you."

"Why?" The simple question slipped from her.

"Because you needed to be rescued."

She met his words with a hysterical laugh before tears flowed anew from her as his words touched her and lifted some of her despair. *Who'd have thought someone cared enough to look for me?*

However, the warmth of his words proved fleeting as a chill ran through her. The reality of what she'd run from crowded her mind. "We have to leave," she sobbed, trying to turn her head and peer into the darkness.

He wouldn't let her glance away. Cupping his hands around her face, he held her gaze. "You're safe now, darling. I won't let anyone hurt you. You have my word on that."

Bailey ignored the inner voice that wondered what he was doing wandering around the woods in just the right place and pretended to not notice the fact he was just as naked as she was. Even amidst her panic and fear, she couldn't help noting his smooth, muscular body pressing against hers, and his . . .

A noise distracted her, and he released her face,

allowing her to turn and peek. Mouth hanging open, and her belly clenching into a now familiar knot of fear, she noted the black wolf that came trotting out of the woods with familiar green eyes. Even in the darkness, she noticed the muzzle appeared matted and damp—*with blood?*

A whimper escaped her, and Gavin stroked his hand soothingly down her back, but that didn't stop her from crying out again as the green-eyed canine was followed out of the gloomy forest by another black-haired wolf and a lighter-coated one. Three wolves converging on her?

A scream finally managed to wend its way past the constrictive barrier of her throat. Terror overwhelmed her, and with exhaustion dogging her, she succumbed to the welcoming darkness.

* * * *

Catching her swooning frame, Gavin thanked every god that might exist for leading him to this particular forest at the right moment, in time to act the knight who rescued his damsel in distress.

They'd only decided on this particular set of woods after tossing a coin. Location decided for the evening's hunt, Gavin and his brothers had driven up in their two SUVS and parked on the country road, a mile or so past the dirt track turnoff leading to where they believed the rogues might have holed up.

There, in the darkness, not even lit by streetlights, they stripped out of their clothing as they prepared to shift to their animal selves, their keener senses as their beasts better suited for a task such as this. As they prepared themselves, they needed no words to communicate. No ribald jokes even peppered the air. They already knew their task in the hunt, and besides, while a car engine would go unnoticed as normal on this lonely stretch of road, conversation, especially at this time of night, wouldn't. They didn't want to announce their presence to rogues who might patrol the woods.

Taking a deep breath, Gavin had called to his inner wolf, a mental exchange that took but a heartbeat. A moment later, the change came over him, and his body reshaped into that of a golden wolf. He'd long ago mastered the pain of shifting, but he wouldn't exactly say it felt great.

Padding off on furry feet, he and his pack mates infiltrated the dark copse of trees, not having to go far before the scent they'd searched for came to them. They split off, loping off into the woods, careful of their steps, and thankfully downwind of those they hunted. Make that the prey his brothers hunted.

Gavin had a slightly different goal—Bailey. He just prayed he didn't find her too late.

Ghosting through the forest, he caught the scent of other Lycans and followed it. Despite his precautions, and surely those of his brothers, who knew how to travel in secret, a warning howl went up by the rogues, their ululating cry lifting into the sky.

Screw stealth. Gavin went for more speed, the thrill of the hunt rousing his beast. He stumbled, though, when he heard a piercing scream, the sound ripping through him and sending his wolf into a frenzy that saw him running full out with no care for himself.

Bailey!

He didn't doubt for one moment the cry came from her. Perking his ears, he listened, straining for a more concrete direction. He caught instead the sound of someone, or something, crashing through the woods with no care that their flight lit a beacon. Then, he heard the harsh gasps and whimpers of a fear so great the mind had come close to shutting down.

Gavin shifted back to his human self just a second before she came tearing through the brush, her head craned back, her naked body a bright slash in the gloomy woods. He stood before her, and still she didn't notice him, running into his sturdy frame and bouncing back. Raising his hands, he steadied her, but in her terror, she didn't look at him.

"Shh, darling. It's okay now. I've got you." His throat closed tight as the sharp scent of her fear enveloped him. A need to protect her surged in him. He would hurt those who had frightened her into this creature of terror. But first, he needed to calm her and get her to safety, right after she stopped fighting him.

Thrashing in his arms, she'd pounded at him, whimpering and crying. He let her vent and tightened the circle of his arms around her, murmuring soft, nonsensical things until she let out a deep sob and stopped fighting.

"G-Gavin?" Her voice emerged as a whisper, broken and uncertain.

"Yes, darling. It's me. I've been looking for you." *Looking my whole life,* because holding her in his arms, her skin touching his, he understood he'd found the one. His mate.

"Why?" The simple question had slipped from her.

"Because you needed to be rescued." *Because I failed you, and I needed to rectify that mistake.*

"We have to leave," she cried.

"You're safe now, darling. I won't let anyone hurt you. You have my word on that." *I will kill them first. No one will ever get to hurt you again. I swear.* So many emotions swamped him in that moment. First and foremost, though, he needed to get her to safety, needed to soothe the terror from her eyes and limbs and calm her until she lost the sharp, fearful aroma that called to all the predators.

A shift in the air currents let Gavin know he was no longer alone as Jaxon slid from the woods, his muzzle wet with blood. Parker and Wyatt soon followed. Apparently, the sight of his pack brothers proved too much for his human mate. With a final shrill scream of terror, she slumped in his arms, the toll of her ordeal too much for her to handle.

Swinging her up into his arms, he enjoyed the lush feel of her and relished even more the relief he'd found her. "I need to get her back to the motel. How many in the woods still?"

Jaxon cocked his head as if thinking and then tapped his paw on the ground one, two, three times.

"Can you and the others take care of it, or should we regroup and call in reinforcements?"

A snort from Wyatt answered that question.

A grin crossed Gavin's lips. "Keep one alive for questioning. I'll see you back at the motel and will expect a full report." He turned to leave, but as he walked away, he tossed a cheerful, "Be careful, puppies."

The short barks of reply made him grin. A part of him wished he could stay behind and mete out a thrashing to the rogues who'd taken Bailey, but he wasn't about to jeopardize her safety just for the satisfaction of hitting something.

It didn't take him long at a quick jog to make it back to the truck. However, he didn't arrive alone. Just as he reached the gravel verge, a mangy cur slunk from the woods, its lip peeled back over its teeth.

"Come to play, have you?" Gavin settled Bailey onto the ground in a patch of weeds before he shifted. This close in succession, and after his sprint through the woods, fatigue pulled at him, but he refused to give in.

Trotting on four feet, he met the rogue's rush in a clash of fur and bodies, the sound of their snarls rising in the night air. It didn't take him long to pin the thug under him, his jaws locked around its throat. The skin in his mouth changed from hairy to human skin, and Gavin joined the rogue in shifting back, panting only slightly from the exertion. His hands replaced his teeth around the man's throat, who eyed him with sweaty and nervous trepidation.

"Who are you?" When the thug didn't immediately answer, Gavin rapped his head off the ground, hard.

A grimace crossed the other man's face. "Leroy."

"Hello there, Leroy. Care to tell me what you and your friends are doing in these woods?"

"Nuttin'."

Letting out a sigh of annoyance, Gavin rolled and picked up the rogue by the throat, his greater strength no match for the scrawny cur. He shook him as Leroy's hands scrabbled at his iron grip.

"Care to rephrase your answer?" Gavin mocked before easing up on the pressure at the man's neck.

Leroy coughed, and his voice emerged raspy. "We was just following orders."

A chill went down Gavin's spine. "Whose orders?"

"I c-c-can't—" Leroy's terrified gaze rolled around, and a keening noise came out of his mouth.

Brow knitted in a frown, Gavin dropped the rogue on the ground. Leroy hit the dirt hard without any attempt to brace his fall. His twitching body shook, and a noise that sounded like . . . laughter emerged from him. With jerky motions, Leroy sat up and faced Gavin, only the whites of his eyes showing.

"Well, well, if it isn't one of Nathan's lackeys." The eerie voice that emerged from Leroy's mouth sent a shiver up Gavin's spine.

"Who are you?"

"What? Didn't my son Nathan tell you?"

"Roderick?" Gavin's query came out high-pitched with incredulity. "That's impossible."

A rusty chuckle made Leroy's body shake, but what Gavin truly found disturbing, apart from the white-orbed gaze, was the trickle of drool tracing its way down the man's chin.

"Stupid dog. And to think I was once as blind as you."

Gavin fought hard not to let his repugnance and discomfiture show. "What do you want with Bailey?"

"Is that the chit's name?" The creature's feigned ignorance didn't fool him. "Nothing anymore, I guess, unless you'd be willing to hand her back. My boys never did get a chance to taste her goods once I tossed her to them. You know she screams quite delightfully."

A roar of rage burst forth from him, and he couldn't prevent his foot from kicking out and smashing into Leroy's face. The rogue went slamming back into the ground, chuckling even as the blood from his broken nose trickled.

"Go ahead and hurt this body. It's not like it belongs to me."

"I'm going to kill you!"

"Yeah, good luck with that. First you'd need to find me."

"I'll make Leroy here tell. Or one of the others."

"You can't make the dead speak."

With those final words, Leroy's body went into convulsions. Gavin took a step toward him and then stumbled back as he watched in horrified fascination the blood pouring from Leroy's eyes and ears. The rogue died with a bubbly wheeze, but Gavin couldn't escape the chill of the encounter.

I need to get Bailey out of here.

Scrounging under the wheel well, he yanked out the magnetic key box and unlocked the SUV. When he picked up Bailey, he found her naked form chilled, but he didn't have time to deal with it. He needed to get her out of here before Roderick changed his mind about her use. Placing her into the backseat, he covered her with a blanket he kept in the trunk for emergencies. He then dressed himself quickly before he hopped in and started the truck.

It took him a moment before he pulled away, a part of him wondering if he should return to aid his pack brothers, but a peek in his rearview mirror made him decide they'd be fine on their own. Or at

Brow knitted in a frown, Gavin dropped the rogue on the ground. Leroy hit the dirt hard without any attempt to brace his fall. His twitching body shook, and a noise that sounded like . . . laughter emerged from him. With jerky motions, Leroy sat up and faced Gavin, only the whites of his eyes showing.

"Well, well, if it isn't one of Nathan's lackeys." The eerie voice that emerged from Leroy's mouth sent a shiver up Gavin's spine.

"Who are you?"

"What? Didn't my son Nathan tell you?"

"Roderick?" Gavin's query came out high-pitched with incredulity. "That's impossible."

A rusty chuckle made Leroy's body shake, but what Gavin truly found disturbing, apart from the white-orbed gaze, was the trickle of drool tracing its way down the man's chin.

"Stupid dog. And to think I was once as blind as you."

Gavin fought hard not to let his repugnance and discomfiture show. "What do you want with Bailey?"

"Is that the chit's name?" The creature's feigned ignorance didn't fool him. "Nothing anymore, I guess, unless you'd be willing to hand her back. My boys never did get a chance to taste her goods once I tossed her to them. You know she screams quite delightfully."

A roar of rage burst forth from him, and he couldn't prevent his foot from kicking out and smashing into Leroy's face. The rogue went slamming back into the ground, chuckling even as the blood from his broken nose trickled.

"Go ahead and hurt this body. It's not like it belongs to me."

"I'm going to kill you!"

"Yeah, good luck with that. First you'd need to find me."

"I'll make Leroy here tell. Or one of the others."

"You can't make the dead speak."

With those final words, Leroy's body went into convulsions. Gavin took a step toward him and then stumbled back as he watched in horrified fascination the blood pouring from Leroy's eyes and ears. The rogue died with a bubbly wheeze, but Gavin couldn't escape the chill of the encounter.

I need to get Bailey out of here.

Scrounging under the wheel well, he yanked out the magnetic key box and unlocked the SUV. When he picked up Bailey, he found her naked form chilled, but he didn't have time to deal with it. He needed to get her out of here before Roderick changed his mind about her use. Placing her into the backseat, he covered her with a blanket he kept in the trunk for emergencies. He then dressed himself quickly before he hopped in and started the truck.

It took him a moment before he pulled away, a part of him wondering if he should return to aid his pack brothers, but a peek in his rearview mirror made him decide they'd be fine on their own. Or at least better off than he currently was alone with an unconscious human.

With a spinning of tires that spat gravel, he shot onto the road, heading for the roadside motel, their newest temporary home during their search. His mind spun chaotically with thoughts of his conversation with Leroy/Roderick, the danger his friends might face, and the woman in the backseat, his mate.

The close quarters of the cab brought her scent to him, and it confused both him and his wolf, for while she smelled more or less as he recalled, if with some kind of harsh soap instead of her honey shampoo, she now had an extra layer to her scent. The aroma tickled at him, for it seemed familiar but kept eluding his grasp.

Reaching the motel they currently called home base—two interconnected rooms at the end of a row—he parked. Checking his surroundings for prying eyes first, he then grabbed the still-unconscious Bailey and carried her into his and Wyatt's room.

She didn't rouse at all, not even when he laid her on the bed. It seemed the perfect opportunity to examine her, not because he was some kind of pervert but because he needed to judge the extent of her injuries, if any. Her body held faint smears of blood, as if from scratches, yet he couldn't see any marks. Perhaps the fluid covered them.

A quick trip to the bathroom and he returned

with a damp cloth, which he stroked over the smooth skin, swallowing hard as he fought the arousal that lifted his cock. She truly was perfect, from her round face with full lips and her crown of dark, curly hair to her lush frame with its indented waist and flaring hips. As he ran the cloth over her rounded belly, he groaned at the exquisite torture of touching her without actually *touching* her.

Oh, darling, I can't wait to make you mine.

A disturbing fact emerged as he cleansed her skin, though, which swept thoughts of seduction from his mind. Dropping the cloth first, he then laid his hands directly on her skin. The simple touch scorched him, but he ignored the sensation as he skimmed his palms over the surface. He lifted her arms, legs, and then rolled her onto her side to look for signs of abuse. Her skin appeared virtually blemish-free, unnaturally so given her mad flight through the woods.

Why doesn't she have any scratches? He lifted her feet to examine them, but while the soles appeared dirty, and he found traces of blood, not a scratch marred their surface.

If he didn't know better, he'd swear her body had healed itself, just as he did, like all Lycans did. *But she's not a wolf.*

What was she then? He stuck his nose down to her skin and inhaled. It just about drove his inner beast mental. The urge to nip her, to sink his teeth in to mark her and taste her blood, starting the claiming process, rode him hard. He restrained himself but only because biting her while she slept didn't exactly seem the right thing to do. No matter if she was his mate or not.

A melody rang out in the silence of the room, startling him. He scooped his cell off the table and answered it with a hushed, "Status?"

Wyatt's voice came across loud and grim. "All dead. We tried to keep one alive like you wanted, but . . . fuck, it's like they just self-destructed. I never saw anything like it before."

"Roderick," Gavin muttered.

"Who?"

"I'll tell you later. Did you find where they were holed up?"

"We're pretty sure we located the place, some abandoned house, but forget finding any clues. The place is a raging inferno. Jaxon almost lost his pretty face when the windows blew out."

In the background, Jaxon piped in, "Chicks dig scars."

Gavin bit back a grin at Wyatt's retorted, "We don't scar, dumbass. Werewolves, remember?" A disgusted sigh preceded Wyatt's next words. "I swear I'm going to get me a silver blade and give him a scar one of these days." Silver was the only material capable of leaving a lasting mark, other than the mating one.

"You guys headed back to the motel?"

"Well duh. Learn anything from Bailey?"

"She's still passed out."

Wyatt grunted. "See you in a few."

"Bye." Gavin hung up and pondered what they'd learned. The rogues were all dead, which was kind of good, as they wouldn't be able to terrorize the surroundings anymore, but bad for them because now they had no clue where Roderick was or what he was up to. Dreading it, Gavin nevertheless rang Nathan, waking the council leader. He quickly relayed the events of the night, which woke their leader up better than a cold nose on the bottom of the feet.

"Fuck. Fuck and fuck." Nathan's language seemed to match the mood of the moment. "You need to bring this girl to us for questioning."

"I don't think she knows anything."

"Whether she does or not isn't relevant. Roderick kidnapped her for a reason. He might have acted like he didn't care about losing her, but it might be a ploy."

Actually, the idea of having Bailey protected within a compound held a lot of appeal. "But what do I tell her about our secret?"

"Nothing until you've claimed her because that is your intention, correct?"

"Yes." How he would accomplish that while keeping his alter ego a secret he wasn't sure, but he'd figure out a way. Although he could always act first and beg forgiveness later.

"We'll head back within the next day then."

"Good. Oh, and, Gavin, be very careful. Roderick is capable of nasty things."

"I know." Gavin hung up and turned back to look at Bailey's still-unconscious form on the bed.

Stroking a finger down her cheek, the only part of her he dared touch with sensual promise. He allowed himself to drink in the sight of her, pushing aside for the moment his questions and anxiety. As if sensing his stare, she finally stirred. She opened her eyes and saw him. Then she screamed.

So much for thinking she feels the same connection. Maybe I should have bitten her first.

Chapter Four

"She's escaped!" His minion, one of his very own creations—after numerous failures—part Lycan, part vampire, burst into his room, eyes blazing and his teeth fully extended.

Such a gauche display, Roderick thought with disdain. "I know."

"Shall I call the dogs together to chase after her?"

Funny how his special minions looked down upon the brethren they'd once belonged to. "Yes. Let the mangy curs out for a run. But tell them if they hurt the girl, I will hurt them ten times worse."

Roderick already knew they wouldn't catch her. After all, he was the one who had orchestrated her escape, planted the seed and compulsion, without her knowledge, of course. He'd wanted his experiment to flee and think she'd slipped his clutches. Like any good Frankenstein daughter, she'd obeyed and run right into the arms of destiny, several pairs of them, he'd bet.

Just call me the puppet master.

Once a wolf, an alpha in charge of a prosperous pack, Roderick despised the depths he'd sunk to, and yet, at the same time, he gloried in his new state of being. Before he'd owned strength, cunning, and an ability to heal that humans could only dream of. Now, he had those same attributes in spades, along with an ability to control weaker minds, a thirst for blood, and a few other skills he'd only just discovered. To date, he'd only had to give up his wolf, and his dignity, to achieve his superior state. Oddly enough, he missed the beast.

To think his own son was the one who had deposed him from his status as alpha. His own flesh and blood who had sent him to the council for justice, and all because he'd protected his pack by killing a few humans.

And yet, with Nathan's daring action, Roderick ended up killing more. The irony of it never failed to amuse him.

Gone to meet his judgment in the form of the Lycan council, Roderick never expected to see his execution transmuted to a living death. Unbeknownst to the packs, the previous Lycan council had spun a deal with a devil, a she-devil, the queen of the vampire covens. Roderick was handed over to her as a gift, the erroneous belief at the time being that wolves could only feed vamps, not become them.

How patently wrong.

Roderick was undead proof that with the right specimen, and lots of torturous pain, a hybrid mix could succeed. Not that the queen celebrated her victory for long. Her powerful blood had sated him for a while when he went into hiding from the covens.

Hiding in the shadows, though, wasn't something Roderick did with ease. *I was meant to wield power.* With that goal in mind, he formed his own coven, or should he say army, not always a willing one, although they were obedient enough once he got hold of their minds and bent them. However, obtaining subjects to convert was proving harder and harder with both the werewolf community and the vampire one hunting him and continually decimating his attempts at building a sizable force.

Death, however, had its benefits, one being longevity, which would come in handy with his new plan, a plan that the escaped Bailey would play an unwitting part in.

The thought of it made him almost giddy, especially knowing when the time turned ripe, just when she thought herself safe and they let their guards down, he'd invoke the bomb he'd secreted.

Through her, he'd get what he wanted most of all and, as an added bonus, enjoy the fireworks of a pack betrayed. And not just the pack but also the council led by Nathan, the ungrateful son who'd started him on his journey to madness—and power.

Chapter Five

Awareness returned, and she stirred, the sheets she laid upon rustling. Bailey froze.

Where am I? Please don't tell me I'm back in that house.

A callused finger stroked down her cheek, and she fought back a whimper. Fear made her keep her eyes clamped shut as she thought furiously. The last thing she recalled, she ran through the woods, pursuit at her heels, and . . . wolves. She remembered the wolf that pounced on her, only to find itself jumped on in return. Then, she recalled running again until she hit a wall.

It wasn't a wall, though, but a chest, a naked chest belonging to—

Wrenching open her eyelids, she came face-to-face with Gavin's clear blue gaze. She couldn't help it. A piercing shriek escaped her.

Rolling sideways, she scrambled off the bed, her feet hitting a carpeted floor. Peering about wildly, she searched for escape or, even better, a weapon. Nothing came immediately to view.

"Calm down." His deep voice washed over her.

Bailey's eyes swiveled to meet his, and she belatedly realized the breathy keening noise came from her.

Holding his hands out, Gavin, now dressed in jeans and a T-shirt, approached her. "Shh, darling. You're safe now. I won't hurt you."

"Ha," she snorted, the sound watery with unshed tears of panic. "Like I'm going to believe you."

As if her words were a sharp dart, his face creased in pain. "I swear it's true. I just want to help you."

"Just how much did you help yourself to already?" The challenging words slipped from her as she peered down at her naked body, searching for a sign he'd molested her while she lay passed out.

Disgust twisted his features. "Give a guy a little credit, would you? You were passed out. Of course I didn't touch you."

"Oh." For some strange reason, his admission deflated her. Did he not find her attractive enough to grope? Probably a good thing considering, good looks or not, there was obviously something wrong with a man who ran around in dark forests wearing only his birthday suit.

"Here, take this." He peeled off his shirt and handed it to her.

Not that she reached out to grab it right away, too mesmerized by the muscular torso he revealed. *Stop staring*, her mind screamed, *before he thinks you're interested.*

But what if she was interested? Her reaction baffled her. Shouldn't she currently scream hysterically having escaped one untenable situation to find herself smack-dab in the middle of an even stranger one? Regardless of how things looked, though, she didn't get a sense of danger from him. Her inner voice remained silent, and a sensation of safety made her tense muscles relax.

However, the illusion of safety didn't mean she should tempt the Fates by staying naked around him.

Snatching the shirt from him, she turned to give him her back while she pulled it on. A low chuckle from behind sent a shiver skating down her spine.

"Kind of late for modesty, don't you think?" he said, humor lacing his remark.

"I know it looks kind of weird, and probably unbelievable given how you found me, but unlike you, I don't usually go cavorting about in the woods naked."

"Why not? I've always found it invigorating myself." He seemed amused by his remark, which she didn't understand.

She whirled around to face him, her modesty appeased by the shirt that hung almost to her knees. "Speaking of which, what were you doing out there in the woods, naked as a jaybird? And how did you find me?"

"Would you believe I was communing with nature?"

"No."

"I'm secretly a werewolf?"

A glare was her reply.

"Yeah, well, I went skinny-dipping with some buddies, and they thought it would be funny to steal my clothes. I was walking through the woods looking for them when you ran into me."

She took a step back, her fear returning. "You're friends with those guys from the house? The ones who wanted to hurt me?"

"What? No!" He appeared angry at her assumption. "I would never stoop to hurting a woman."

"But you know of them?"

"I did after I found you. It seems those *men* weren't too eager to let you go. My friends and I taught them otherwise."

A tremble skated through her at the implied violence in his words. "What about the other girl? The one at the house? Was she rescued too?"

A frown knitted his brow. "What other girl?"

"The one I heard crying."

"I don't know anything about another girl, darling, I'm sorry. Are you sure you're not mistaken?"

"No—I—" She shut her mouth and tried to think back. *Is it possible it was just me?* The memories of the night floated hazily in her mind, probably an aftereffect of the drugs they'd given her to get her out of the bar. But still, she thought she'd heard someone else crying in that ramshackle house, and she'd seen that thug come out of a room buckling his pants. However, she'd never actually seen another girl, just assumed from the evidence she'd witnessed. "Maybe I was mistaken. Did you call the cops?"

A blank mask dropped over his face. "No. Do you really want to deal with their bureaucratic crap? I mean you escaped before you got hurt, and we took care of the guys who abducted you."

His evasion made her uneasy. True, she didn't want to get stuck in some police station being questioned for hours, but still, a crime had been committed. "But what if they decide to kidnap someone else because I didn't turn them in?"

"Oh, they won't be trying anything like that ever again. That I can promise you." Dark menace made his eyes flash, and his lips curled into a humorless smile.

A shiver traveled down her spine. "What did you do?"

"Me? Nothing but get you out of there, and smack someone called Leroy. My buddies, though, they're quite handy with their fists, and they took exception to the actions of those scumbags."

Strangely, a savage satisfaction filled her at the thought those thugs, Leroy in particular, had gotten the daylights beaten out of them. The harder, the better.

What's happening to me? Since when did she revel in violence or find it acceptable? She needed to get out of here, back to her place, where she could shower and think over the unreal events of the past evening, sort them and figure out why it seemed as if she should recall something else—something important that skittered just out of reach. "I need to go home."

"I don't think that's wise," he replied.

Narrowing her eyes, she tried to read his expression, but while he returned her gaze, his face appeared shuttered. "Why not? I thought you said those guys were gone, which means I'm safe."

Gavin scrubbed a hand through his hair, the blond tufts standing on end and making him look deliciously rumpled, a fact she shouldn't have noticed under the circumstances. "They are, but we have reason to believe they weren't working alone."

For a moment, she stopped breathing. "What are you talking about? What do you mean, not working alone?"

"Exactly what I said. I don't think you're safe because I think the guys we caught aren't the only ones involved."

"So we call the cops, and they protect me."

"The cops aren't going to do a damned thing because there's nothing for them to investigate."

"Okay, now you're not making any sense. I can tell them what happened."

"Tell them what? That you woke up in a house with two guys? You don't have a mark on you. You don't remember a thing. What exactly do you think the cops will do?"

His logic irritated her, especially since the more she thought about it, the less she wanted to deal with the police. One part of his argument, though, took a second to sink in. "What do you mean I don't have a mark on me? I fell down the stairs and then ran naked through the woods. I must be covered in bruises and scra . . ." Her voice trailed off as she took stock of the fact that not a single part of her body ached. She plopped her bottom on the bed and lifted her feet to peer at her soles, which, while dirty, showed no signs she'd cut and scratched them during her mad flight.

It makes no sense. But it did remind her of the incident in the bedroom with the bloody cut. *What's happening to me?*

She wanted the comfort of her familiar space more than ever. "I want to go home."

"No." He said it quietly in a tone that said he wouldn't budge.

"You can't stop me." She took a step toward him.

Muscular arms crossed over his bare chest. "Actually, I can. In case you haven't noticed, I'm a tad bigger than you. Good luck going through me."

"So now I'm a prisoner again, am I?"

"Think of it more as a protective measure."

"Says you. I say, screw you. I'm leaving, and you'd better not try to stop me."

Bailey marched over to the door, which she hoped led outside, and pulled it open. Then she looked up, and up again, at the man sporting the extremely wide chest blocking her way.

"And where do you think you're going?" the brick wall asked.

"Crazy apparently," she mumbled, stumbling back. "I swear this whole evening is getting weirder and weirder."

"Evening? I would have thought you'd have said days," the brown-eyed giant replied.

An icy chill spread through her. "What do you mean days?"

"Ah shit."

Bailey whirled to look at Gavin. "What's he talking about? How long since you and I met at that bar?"

He shifted uncomfortably. "Five nights ago."

"Five!" That did it. Her eyes rolled up in her head, and she slumped to the ground in a faint.

* * * *

Parker caught the little lady before she hit the ground while ignoring Gavin's glare. It wasn't hard, not with the plush form of the most delectable-smelling female he'd ever met. No wonder her disappearance had driven Gavin nuts. This close to her, Parker couldn't deny her appeal—or his immediate attraction to her, a pull also felt by his inner wolf, which paced in agitation.

"What did you go and tell her that for?" Gavin's irritation—and jealousy—came through loud and clear.

Parker managed to flip him a bird while carrying the limp Bailey to the bed. "I didn't realize it was a big deal."

"Neither did I," Gavin replied, his shoulders slumping. "I realized as soon as she woke up and started talking that she'd lost track of time."

Eyeing her frame, his gaze taking its time perusing her up and down, especially her plump thighs peeking from the edge of the T-shirt, an urge to cover her body with his made his cock swell. *What is it about her that intrigues me?* Inhaling deeply, he let the scent of her sift through his senses. His teeth lengthened as his wolf abruptly pushed forward. Clamping his control down tight, Parker moved back a step and frowned. "What is she?"

"You smell something different too?"

"Not pack, and yet . . ." Parker inhaled again. "There's something about her, something familiar. But at the same time—"

"There's an aroma of something not quite right. Not human, and not her. I know. It's been driving me nuts. Want to hear something weirder? She didn't smell like this five days ago."

That grabbed Parker's attention. "What do you mean she smelled different? Could those bastards have marked her, or worse?"

"I found no signs of rape," Gavin replied, coming over to stand across from him on the other side of the bed.

"Even stranger, there's not a single mark on her

body."

"Five days and they didn't touch her?" Incredulity made Parker's eyes shoot from the girl's form to his friend's.

"Not even a tiny scratch from the woods I caught her racing through."

The information hit Parker, but before he could assimilate it, the door to the motel flung open. Wyatt stalked in, followed by a sauntering Jaxon.

"Did you get any answers?" Wyatt growled, purposely ignoring Bailey to grab himself a can of pop from the mini-fridge.

"None that you're going to like," Gavin replied.

"I don't think she's one hundred percent human," Parker blurted.

Three pairs of eyes swiveled to fix him.

"Explain," Wyatt said curtly.

"Sniff for yourself. She doesn't smell exactly like wolf, but she's got something in her blood. How else to explain her lack of injuries?"

Wyatt wasn't the only one crowding in for a whiff. Jaxon jostled in beside Gavin, who hip-checked him to the side. Stumbling, their youngest pack mate grinned and sidled over to stand beside Parker. Parker didn't bother resisting the urge to taste her aroma again. He leaned in with his pack brothers and let himself enjoy the musky scent that teased him.

For a few minutes, silence reigned in the room as they each allowed themselves to filter the bouquet of her scent. The only audible admission that Bailey was more than just any woman appeared in the increased heart rate for each of them—even Wyatt.

One by one, they moved away from her, Parker seating himself on the motel's sturdy faux leather chairs while Jaxon hopped up onto the dresser. Gavin and Wyatt remained standing, wearing troubled frowns.

"Parker's right. Something about her is off."

"But she didn't smell like that the night we met her, though, right?" Gavin queried.

Wyatt's mouth tightened into a thin line. "I don't know. I wasn't really interested in pinpointing her scent at the time. But at the same time, I've never heard of someone's smell changing."

"Or how about the fact she might have gone from human to something new?" Jaxon piped in.

"Like what, smart-ass?"

Parker bit back a grin as Wyatt turned his formidable glare on Jaxon, who just shrugged and grinned. At times it was hard to tell who led their group, Gavin with his laid-back ways or Wyatt with his single-mindedness when it came to tasks.

"No need to kill me with your killer laser gaze. I'm just saying, if it's possible for Roderick, Nathan's dad, to turn into a vampire, then who's to say there's not other things out there that we don't know about?"

A grin stretched Parker's face. "I hate to say this, but the pup might have a point. If we believe

Nathan and the whole undead thing, then why not humans turning into yummy-smelling things? I mean, none of us are disputing the fact there's something odd about her, right?"

"And I get the impression I'm not the only one whose beast is chomping at the bit to take a bite," Gavin added.

"Awoo!" howled Jaxon before laughing as he ducked the pillow sent his way by Wyatt.

"Enough screwing around. And shut up a bit, or do you want her waking up and hearing us talking crazy?"

The thought of freaking Bailey out sobered them instantly. Parker's eyes flicked over to her where she still slumbered on the bed. The idea of marking a woman had never crossed his mind before. Then again, he'd never come across one who made him want to bay at the moon.

However enticing her pheromones, it didn't mean fate had earmarked her for him. Looking down at her again, Parker bit back a sigh as his wolf howled in his mind. Okay, maybe she was, but to become her mate, he'd first need her to get past the fact that, at six foot seven, he stood taller than most men and that his bulk was solidly muscled. Her first reaction upon seeing him didn't exactly encourage him. Ignoring the physical aspect, judging by his pack brothers' reaction, he'd also have to resign himself to the fact that he'd have to share her, with Jaxon and Gavin at the very least. With Wyatt, he still couldn't be sure because, when it came to duty, Parker doubted Wyatt would let a woman get in his way, mate or not. Of course, all this assumed Bailey would want to share her affections with more than one man. Most human females didn't.

While pack law dictated Lycan females needed to mate with at least a pair of males of her choice, human females weren't subject to their laws. Despite what their wolves wanted, if Bailey chose one, they'd have to abide by her decision. Did he stand a chance if it came to him competing with his brothers?

Of course all this musing might be moot. She could wake up and hate us all on sight, or have the personality of a shrew.

Somehow, though, he got the feeling Bailey would end up just right.

"So what's our next move?" Wyatt asked.

"I can think of a few," Jaxon piped in with a swirl of his hips.

Parker snorted as both Gavin and Wyatt shot the pup a glare.

"Now we take her somewhere safe. Back home, to the pack."

Chapter Six

The next time she woke, Bailey feigned sleep and listened to . . . nothing. She let out her pent-up breath. It embarrassed her to know she'd fainted, but the shock over discovering she'd gone missing for five days still made her tremble.

What happened to me?

That question kept repeating itself over and over in her mind. A blank slate met her mental queries. Could Gavin and his friend have lied? Possibly, after all, what did she know of her blond cowboy and his friends? Up to this point, she'd assumed he told her the truth, but what if he deceived her? Perhaps he belonged to the plot to kidnap her and had simply lulled her into thinking he was her savior.

If that were the case, then she was in big freaking trouble. Yet, her inner radar for danger remained silent. Should she trust her gut or her mental musings?

Frustration made her grunt and roll over, forgetting for a moment her situation. Eyes still clamped tight, she froze, feigning sleep just in case she wasn't alone, a sham that didn't fool anyone.

A wry voice spoke. "Too late. I know you're awake."

Prying open one eyelid, she managed not to shriek as she noticed the dark-haired stranger from the bar sitting in a chair across from her. He still appeared just as darkly good-looking, with a bit of rough stubble along his jaw that enhanced his full lips, which pulled into a tight line at her perusal.

"Just how many bloody friends does the cowboy have anyway?" she grumbled as she sat up. She noted she still wore the T-shirt Gavin had given her so assumed no molestation had occurred, unless they'd kept her clothed. But judging by how she felt—neither sticky nor sore—she assumed they'd left her alone.

Probably because I'm not their type. Good-looking guys like that must have the hottest, and skinniest, girls crawling all over them.

One short and chubby plain Jane obviously didn't come across as an irresistible temptation and gave credence to Gavin's statement that he'd rescued her by happenstance.

"There's four of us. I'm Wyatt. You've met Gavin, fainted for Parker, and will, unfortunately, at one point, make Jaxon's acquaintance."

"What are you? A gang of some kind?"

A tilt to his lips made her heart hitch because, awake and looking at him full on, she couldn't help notice that this stranger, Wyatt, appeared quite attractive in his own right. Where Gavin was blond and blue-eyed, Wyatt seemed descended from Native American roots, with his blue-sheened black hair and dark, piercing gaze. His skin tone appeared tan, that or he was naturally swarthy. A curious part of her wondered, when he took off his shirt, if that smooth, buttery skin would extend to below his waistband. She almost slapped herself at the thought.

Now is not the time to lust after handsome strangers.

"We prefer the term 'pack,' actually. But enough about our boring group. Gavin tells me you want to go home."

"Yes." She practically hopped out of the bed. "Will you take me? Gavin said it was too dangerous."

For a moment, he just stared at her, and she could have sworn she saw another presence behind his eyes, a *hungry* one. Nonsense, of course, but it didn't stop a prickling sensation from spreading through her. Yet, she didn't get the sense of any danger.

"It might be a tad perilous, but with me and the boys at your side, you should be safe enough."

Bailey's smile wilted. "Don't tell me you're buying into this whole conspiracy thing. I mean a couple of guys slipped me a Mickey. Happens all the time."

"And the five days you've been missing?"

Red eyes bored into hers while cadaverous fingers . . .

She shook her head. "No. I don't believe it. I don't know what you and your friends' game is, but I'm not buying it. I mean look at me. Don't you think if I'd been held prisoner for five days, I'd have some injuries to show for it?"

"I have been looking, and I'll admit, I'm baffled. So why don't you tell me how you healed them?"

She gaped at him. "Oh my God. You're just as loony as the rest of them. Healed them?" She giggled, perhaps a little too shrilly, as the memory of her disappearing scratch from the derelict house came back to haunt her.

She refused to believe her recollection. It had to be the drugs that made her think she'd injured herself and miraculously healed. Anything else . . . was just plain nuts.

A snort was his reply to her mirth. "Whatever, sunshine. Here." He tossed her some fabric, and she caught it, her brow knitting until she realized he'd given her some track pants. "Get dressed. We're leaving."

"Turn around," she ordered.

With a sigh of annoyance, he gave her his back, a very broad back that pulled at the fabric of his shirt.

Tugging on the pants, she noticed they didn't fit, at all, and she had to roll the cuffs as well as yank the drawstrings as tight as possible. Not exactly an attractive look, but at least she wasn't bare-assed anymore.

"Now what? Are you taking me home, or am I calling a cab?"

He didn't answer her at first, instead opening the door to stick his head out and loosing a sharp whistle. He then whirled around and fixed her with a dark stare that she began to recognize as his natural state. "We'll drive you. But I warn you, home isn't the haven you're looking for."

Irritated at his cool manner, she stuck her tongue out at him in a childish gesture of defiance then immediately regretted it as his placid mask slipped. For a moment, his eyes seemed to blaze, and his lips curled into a taunting smile.

"Careful, sunshine, or I might just put that thing to good use."

Bailey clamped her lips tight, but she couldn't stop the coiling warmth that settled low in her belly at his words. *Perhaps he's not so cold after all.* She didn't know if she liked that or not.

In silence, she followed him outside, her bare feet making only a whisper of sound as she hit the concrete walkway outside the motel door. She noted the sun shone brightly, and she peered up at the sky to see it just rising from the east, placing the time around early morning. Bringing her gaze back down, she saw Wyatt had left her and stood by the open door of a large black SUV.

Grimacing at the gravel that separated her from him, she placed one tentative foot on the rough surface.

"Bloody hell." Wyatt no sooner muttered the expletive than he returned to her side and scooped her in his arms. Startled at her sudden loss of balance, she flailed her arms wildly before clinging to him.

"I'm not going to drop you," he murmured, the first hint of humor finally edging his tone.

"Says you. I know I'm not a lightweight," she retorted.

"A woman should have curves, so I'd say you're just about right," he replied, surprising her before he dumped her into the backseat of the truck. Before she could answer, or even assimilate his compliment, he'd slammed the door shut and clambered into the front. Peeking forward, she found her attention snagged by a familiar face.

"Gavin!"

"Hey, darling."

"Are you guys really taking me home?"

"Yeah, but I don't think you'll want to stay," he replied cryptically.

"That's what you think," she grumbled, leaning back in the seat and watching the scenery fly by. She didn't engage them in further conversation, preferring not to let their craziness infect her. Although she feared it was too late. The closer they got to her apartment, the more the tension mounted inside her. Her inner voice growled without words in her head, the meaning clear. *Danger.*

When they pulled up in front of her building, realization struck. "I don't have my keys." She didn't have a single item left from her sojourn to the bar before her abduction.

"Yes, you do." Gavin turned around and handed

her the purse she'd thought lost.

A suspicious glare shot his way made him chuckle. "Put those daggers away. We found it outside of the bar, in the parking lot."

"Oh." She flashed him a sheepish grin. Clutching tightly at her purse, her nervousness mounting, she didn't know what to say next, so she settled for something trite. "Well, thanks for the ride."

Wyatt snorted before he climbed out. "You're not getting rid of us that easily." Seeing him at her door, she slid across the seat to get to the other side, but Wyatt, his reach long, snagged her and yanked her out.

"Hey. Put me down."

"Would you stop acting up? You're going to draw the wrong kind of attention."

"Maybe that's what I want," she snapped, but she did stop struggling, especially when she saw Gavin perusing their surroundings with suspicion. When Wyatt deposited her inside the vestibule for her building, she didn't run. Why bother? They'd probably just follow.

Given the cold of the tile floor, she almost wished she'd kept her mouth shut and let him carry her farther, but she wouldn't ask. Holding her head high, trying to act as if she were alone and not wearing men's ill-fitting castoffs, she strode the length of the short hall to the elevator and stabbed the button.

A tingling sensation at her back let her know

without turning that Gavin and Wyatt both followed. The knowledge warmed her and eased some of her trepidation. The elevator arrived, and she stepped in then moved back as two large male bodies crowded in after her. They didn't ask her what floor, but Wyatt unerringly hit the button for the correct one.

Bailey caught her lower lip between her teeth. *This makes no sense. Why isn't my inner warning bell going off?* These guys knew way too many things about her and her disappearance, yet here she went along with them blithely.

She felt no panic in their presence, although she did have a pile of mounting questions. Starting with, why did their proximity make her heart race and her cleft moisten? Not just for Gavin but for Wyatt too. *I'm turning into a slut.* Odd, because she'd never owned a high sex drive before. Sex was something she did to please her boyfriend, not because she got that much out of it.

Ignoring them in an attempt to calm her burgeoning interest didn't work because they smelled so damned good. She'd never noticed a man's scent before, but now, stuck in a small box with them, she couldn't help breathing it in. Absorbing it. Enjoying it . . .

The ding of the elevator snapped her out of a sensual olfactory feast, and she raised her gaze to see them both staring at her.

"Soon, darling." Gavin's softly spoken words

whispered over her skin like a caress.

Cheeks blossoming with color, she wondered if they'd somehow caught on to her interest. How embarrassing.

She ducked her head to their low chuckles.

"Hallway looks clear. I'll take point."

Gavin took the lead down the hall while Wyatt stuck to her rear. It shouldn't have surprised her when her blond cowboy stopped right outside her door, but it did. Just how many secrets did they keep?

"Keys?" he questioned.

Startled from her distrustful musings, she rummaged in her purse for them. It was with cold and clammy fingers that Bailey inserted her key into the lock, the sense of wrongness increasing.

The door opened onto chaos, and Bailey walked in, her mind numb with shock.

"What happened to my home?" she cried, wading through the mess. Everywhere she looked, destruction reigned, with her couch slashed to ribbons, paper shredded all over, and glass, from her kitchenware, littering the place. She didn't even want to contemplate what the various runny stains on the walls were. And the stench. She gagged, and brought a hand up to her nose.

"They came back," Wyatt stated grimly.

Stunned, Bailey didn't resist when Gavin tugged at her body so she faced him. Blue eyes, dark with concern, stared into hers. "We need to leave, darling."

"No, we need to call the cops," she said through lips gone numb with shock. "These jerks can't get away with trashing my home and kidnapping me. I don't care about the paperwork. These guys need to pay." The more the reality of the crime sunk in, the more she found herself burning with a need for revenge.

"The police won't catch them," Wyatt replied in an acerbic tone.

Whirling, Bailey fixed Wyatt with a glare. "So what do you suggest I do? Wait until they come back? Move away and live in fear, wondering if they'll follow?"

"Neither. You're coming with us," Wyatt announced.

Shrill laughter bubbled from her. "Like hell. I don't know who the heck you and your friends think you are, but I am not going anywhere with you. And I suggest you leave before the cops show up because I'm calling them whether you like it or not." Bailey waded through the detritus, in the direction of a side table, in the hopes of finding her phone.

A thick forearm circled her waist and yanked her back.

"I'm sorry, Bailey, but Wyatt is right. You can't stay here. You need to come with us. There are things going on that I can't explain. But trust me when I say it's dangerous for you to stay. We can keep you safe."

Pushing at the arm manacling her didn't budge it. "Let me go. I'm not going anywhere with you guys." She opened her mouth to shriek, but a hand clamped over it.

Thrashing now in earnest, Bailey fought to escape Gavin's grip, which proved useless. The man was solid as a rock and just as immovable. In the midst of her struggles, she glimpsed Wyatt watching while shaking his head, his lips tight.

"We can't carry her out in broad daylight fighting like a rabid vixen."

Bailey proved Wyatt's point by stomping down on Gavin's foot.

"And what would you suggest we do?" Gavin asked through gritted teeth. "We can't stay here, and I'm not leaving her."

"Are you that sure?"

"Yes, damn it. And besides, Nathan wants to see her."

Bailey's fight lessened as she listened to their cryptic conversation.

"Mark her. That'll at least bind her to you so that she's more likely to trust."

"But she's unwilling." Gavin's voice sounded unhappy.

"Oh, please," Wyatt snorted. "We both know it's going to happen at one point anyway. Remember what my dad used to say?"

"It's easier to beg for forgiveness than ask permission from a woman."

Ha, like she'd ever forgive Gavin, or Wyatt, for that matter, for treating her as if she didn't own a choice.

Wyatt laughed. "My dad, the fountain of knowledge. Do it. We'll worry about the rest later, when we've got her stashed safely away in the heart of the pack. Besides, didn't Nathan say no secrets revealed until you did?"

"I remember what Nathan said, but you know how Dana feels about forcing a claim."

"So we take the long road back so it's not an issue by the time we arrive."

Gavin sighed. "I still don't like this."

"But?"

"I'll do it." Gavin's lips brushed up against her ear as he whispered, "I'm sorry, Bailey, but you leave me no choice."

That sounded ominous, even if she didn't understand what their entire byplay meant. She renewed her struggles, but Wyatt came to stand in front of her. His added strength kept her still while Gavin used one hand to brush the hair from her nape. The hand over her mouth still muffled her, and she thought about biting it, anything to help free the frantic mumbles of her trapped scream.

Warm lips touched her skin at the back of her shoulder, a soft caress that even amidst the turmoil triggered an answering response in her body.

"I will make this up to you, from this day forth, for the rest of our lives. Believe me when I say, one day you'll understand what I'm doing and thank me for it."

A shiver went down her spine at his odd pronouncement. Before she could ponder it further, Gavin opened his mouth wide on her skin, the tip of his longue laving her, and then . . . he bit her hard enough to break skin.

Bailey screeched at the sudden pain of it, and it was reflex for her to chomp down on the hand over her mouth. She bit a little too hard and punctured his skin, not that he flinched or moved away. On the contrary, he emitted a growl and sucked more intently at her neck while the coppery taste of his blood filled her mouth.

Appalled, she tried to stem the flow of blood with her tongue, but the fluid, with no place to go, filled her mouth. She panicked as the realization struck that she had to swallow or she'd choke on his blood.

Grossed out, but the need for survival stronger, she gulped Gavin's blood down, her eyes screwed tight. And at the first gulp, lightning hit.

* * * *

Blood to blood. Soul to soul. Gavin felt the connection forge between them, an almost tangible link that would join him to Bailey until death parted them. Even given the circumstances, the power behind it awed him.

Most matings occurred during sex, and Gavin could easily see why, given the rigidity of his cock. The urge to bury himself inside of her, claiming her with his body, and not just his soul, rode him hard. As he licked the spot he'd bitten, he couldn't help rubbing himself against her backside. Shock swept through him when she gyrated back against him with a moan. Despite her reluctance to trust, she obviously felt the same pull. *Of course she does. She's my mate.*

His mate. And he'd yet to even kiss her.

Not for long.

He let his hand slide from her mouth, ready to return it if she screamed, but instead, she sighed as he turned her in his arms. She came willingly, her eyes glazed with wonder, and when he fitted his mouth to hers, the world around them disappeared until only she remained. His new reason for being, his woman, his mate.

Slanting his mouth eagerly over hers, he took what she offered and demanded more. Clutched tightly to him, she felt so right, her plush frame a perfect complement to his hardness. He lifted her off the ground so she wouldn't have to crane, and she mewled in need, clutching at his shoulders, a sound that rose in intensity when he ground himself against her hidden core.

A throat cleared. "Um, I hate to interrupt, but we need to leave."

Reluctance made him want to ignore his friend's words, but his new duty to his mate took precedence. Her safety was more important than his lust.

Gavin tore his lips from hers and allowed himself a moment to stare down at her upturned face. "So beautiful," he murmured, seeing her kiss-swollen lips, flushed cheeks, and bright eyes. "Come, my darling. We will continue this elsewhere."

"Wha-What just happened?" she asked, a crease marring her brow. "What did you just do to me?"

"He claimed you. He can explain what that means later. For now, let's get out of here before those rogues return and force us to fight." Wyatt's words broke the sensual spell, but did nothing to dispel the confusion on her face.

"Rogues? I don't—"

It seemed natural to hush her with a kiss, to which Wyatt snorted and rolled his eyes. Despite his friend's attempts at nonchalance, though, Gavin could see the envy—and desire—in his gaze. He'd bet his last dollar it wouldn't be long before Wyatt asked Bailey to allow him a bite.

The thought pleased Gavin, his earlier jealousy at sharing melted now that he'd claimed her. *If I have to share her with anyone, I would hope it would be my best friend, and almost brother.*

A shake of his head, and Wyatt once again wore his smooth mask. "Bring her to the truck while I see if I can salvage any of her clothes and stuff. I'll meet you down there in five minutes."

Letting Bailey up for air, Gavin heard her complain. "Wait. I never agreed to go. And—"

Gavin kissed her again. It was his pleasure to do so, and to his gratification, each time he did, she melted in his arms. The only problem with all the embraces was the effect on his poor cock, which throbbed unhappily behind his thick denim.

Arm anchored around her side, he waltzed her out of the apartment, brushing his lips across hers whenever she opened her mouth to protest. It wasn't until they reached the elevator that he released her lips so she could speak.

"Just because you're a good kisser doesn't mean you're allowed to kidnap me," she informed him breathlessly.

"Only good?" he teased with an arched brow. A red hue flushed her cheeks, and he grinned.

"Stop trying to distract me. I want to know what's going on. Really going on."

"I want to tell you. Believe me I do. But for now, you need to trust me."

Messy, dark curls went flying as she shook her head. "How can I trust you when I barely know you? Everything is moving so fast, and I don't understand anything."

"The only thing you need to know right now is that you are very important to me, and I need to make sure you're safe."

A long sigh escaped her, almost drowned by the ding of the elevator arriving at the main floor of her building.

"I wish I could believe you."

The doors slid open, and before he could discern her intent, she thrust her knee into his groin. He sucked in a startled breath, and she shoved him off-balance before she took off running. It took him only seconds to regain his balance, and he tore after her. He hit the door for the exit, rebounding from the glass surface before he managed to locate the release clasp to open it. Those few seconds cost him and gave her a head start that proved enough to hide her from him when he hit the sidewalk.

Eyes scanning rapidly, he searched the almost deserted area but didn't catch any signs of movement.

Obviously, she'd turned off into an alley nearby or building. But which one? He sniffed the air, catching a trace of her scent to the . . .

A scream, abruptly cut off, sent him running into the alley bordering her building. Skidding around the corner, he came across Bailey struggling in the grip of a stranger while another advanced on her menacingly with something in his hand. Gavin dashed toward them, his heart racing as he wondered if he could make it in time.

Thankfully, Parker strolled into sight at the bottom end of the alley, just steps from the bastards.

"Put her down," his giant friend demanded in a soft tone.

The thug, holding what Gavin now recognized as a syringe, turned with a belligerent, "Or else what?"

"Are you fucking kidding me?" Parker shook his head. "Man, you rogues are dumb as shit. Jaxon, get the girl while I teach these dicks a lesson in how to treat a lady."

From behind Parker, Jaxon sprinted forward while Gavin raced to meet them from the back. Their pack giant, Parker, lashed out at the thug wielding the needle, but instead of moving away from the swing, the rogue stood there and took it, the force of it propelling him into a heap on the ground at Bailey's feet.

Gavin only had time to yell, "No," before the rogue plunged the syringe into Bailey's leg and depressed the plunger. Too late, Parker, with a roar, grabbed the thug and tossed him away. In the chaos, Jaxon jumped onto the thug holding Bailey. A few cuffs to the rogue's ear, and Bailey was released to slump, with glazed eyes, to the ground.

When the guy Parker pummeled came flying his way, Gavin caught him and spun him, pressing him up against the wall with an arm over his throat.

"Who the fuck are you?" he growled as his wolf pushed at his control.

"One of many," replied the rogue with a lunatic grin before his eyes rolled up in his head and he began to thrash. Gavin dropped him and stepped back, chilled at the ease with which Roderick disposed of his minions.

"Hey, bro. Lose your woman?"

Whirling, Gavin found Jaxon holding Bailey in his arms while Parker made a moue of distaste at the other rogue, who convulsed on the ground.

"What the fuck just happened?" his giant friend asked.

"Roderick. It seems he's not about to leave any loose ends for us to question. Quick. We need to get out of here before someone calls the cops."

"Where's Wyatt?" Jaxon asked, leading the way with Gavin's mate.

It took some willpower to resist the jealous urge to snatch her from his friend. She was his mate. His.

It should have fallen on him, the job of rescuing and then carrying his woman. But he controlled his base urge to smack the pup upside the head. It wouldn't do to start a pissing contest yet when he'd seen the interest in Jaxon's eyes that said, along with Wyatt and Parker, Gavin might find himself in a four-way pack mating.

That will be a first for someone not Lycan born.

He'd only ever heard of one human bond having a pair of wolves. Then again, doubt remained as to what exactly Bailey was. None of this had anything to do with the problems at hand, though. Time to get his mind back on his pack brothers and getting out of there before more rogues appeared.

"I'll get Wyatt. You guys get Bailey out of here. We'll rendezvous at the squirrel place."

Gavin didn't speak the name of the place aloud in case hidden ears listened. Parker, though, caught the reference as he swung behind the wheel of the SUV while Jaxon slid into the back with Bailey on his lap.

"Take care of her," he added, drinking in the sight of her, hopefully not his last.

"Don't worry, man. I'll keep her nice and warm for you." Jaxon laughed as Gavin growled, his lunge hitting the truck door just as Jaxon pulled it shut.

"I'll make sure the puppy behaves," Parker rumbled. "Be careful."

The SUV pulled away, and Gavin watched the taillights for a moment before jogging back to the building, in search of his pack brother. Debating on whether to go through the rear or front, he ended up choosing neither as Wyatt emerged from the building shaking his head.

"We'll need to hit a store. Those bastards pissed on everything she owned, even her fucking shoes."

"We've got bigger problems." Gavin relayed the events of the past few minutes as they clambered into their own truck and sped away.

"Shit," Wyatt cursed. "What the hell is so goddamned special about her?"

Other than the fact she makes my heart race, my cock throb, and my mind whirl? "I don't know. But we need to find out. And fast."

Chapter Seven

Jaxon couldn't help stroking the smooth cheek of the female nestled on his lap. Sure, he could have dumped her onto the seat and joined Parker up front to ride shotgun, but he worried she'd roll onto the floor. Okay, he lied. He could have buckled her in to keep her safe. The truth was, he just didn't want to let her go.

From the moment he'd first inhaled her scent in the motel room, he'd found himself intrigued—and harder than a teenage boy with his first issue of *Playboy*. She wasn't bimbo beautiful, like his usual conquests, but Jaxon couldn't say he'd ever seen a more appealing woman.

She possessed lush curves covered in creamy skin that begged stroking. Her wild, curly hair tumbled about her face and shoulders, giving her the look of a woman just roused—or loved. Her bowed mouth, so full and tempting, was made to suck cock, and he could only imagine what a striking contrast she'd make, naked, against his own dark skin.

Shifting her on his lap, and away from his wakening dick, he noted the mating mark on the back of her neck, which, by its scent, belonged to Gavin. It didn't surprise him given how madman-like Gavin had acted since her disappearance. And where their alpha leader went, so did

Wyatt. Although, if Jaxon had him pegged right, Wyatt would fight his attraction to Bailey tooth and nail. The man never did take the easy way or let anything interfere with what he called his "responsibilities." *I'll bet he's never tried taking on fate, though. But you know what they say, the harder they fight, the more naked they fall.*

A snicker escaped him, and he pretended not to see Parker's frown in the rearview mirror. He figured the big guy would also hone in on the action because he'd seen Parker's interest in her, which he found intriguing because Parker never seemed to notice women. The thought of the lush Bailey bouncing atop the behemoth was enough to make him go cross-eyed. He did so love a good show.

Visual erotic fun aside, though, that made three possible mates for the human who was something more, which left just enough room for him to complete the group—if the other three didn't throttle him first.

It didn't escape him that he drove his pack brothers nuts. He kind of did so on purpose, loving to see the guys he'd idolized growing up going apeshit. At three years younger than Parker, and five from Gavin and Wyatt, he sometimes despaired of them ever seeing him as anything less than the little kid who used to follow them around. But as his mama always told him, *"One step at a time."* He'd managed to get appointed to their hunting group, slowly befriended them, and now, if the lady in question were agreeable, he'd spend his life with them as one of Bailey's mates.

If that happens, I wonder if I can talk them into a fivesome? Wanna bet that particular suggestion gets my face rearranged? A shame, though, because having grown up in a polygamous society where the women took on more than one mate, he'd also heard the stories of polyamorous matings, tag team sex, so to speak, that brought all the players closer—but not touching each other. He might like watching couples fuck, but he preferred pussy to dick.

Jaxon's sexual escapades, while many and varied, never got any more numerous, or wild, than with two girls. Even he admitted it wasn't exactly the same as a group orgy with one woman as the focus of several guys. His curiosity wasn't because he was bi or interested in men at all, but because he had a bit of a voyeuristic streak. Sure, he loved to plow a woman's wet sex, his body heaving and straining for that orgasmic fulfillment, but he'd discovered over the years he also loved to watch. Nothing beat seeing the expression on her face as she got it from behind or watching the pumping action of a cock as it thrust into a waiting pussy, all visual pleasures he'd gotten via video thus far.

Looking down at Bailey's serene, drug-induced face, he wondered if he'd found the woman who would help fulfill his fantasy, who would accept him as a man and not make him continually prove himself like his pack mates. *A mate to love me.*

"Hey, puppy, what's got you so quiet back there?"

"Just thinking about how hungry I am," Jaxon replied. "For some hot pussy pie."

"Idiot. Don't you dare go getting designs on the little lady. If my nose is correct, she's spoken for."

"I can smell that. So what if she already chose Gavin? Pack law says she can have up to three more."

Parker's brown eyes lifted to catch his in the rearview mirror. "And the new law states that she gets to choose."

"I know, which is why I intend to court her."

"Get in line, then, because I know this woman is meant to be my mate, and I get the feeling, despite his attitude, that Wyatt's going to be vying for her attention."

"Which leaves just enough room for me as her fourth."

"You're either brave or nuts to want to join yourself with us for the rest of your life. You do know Wyatt's likely to kill you if you ever step over the line."

"Bah," Jaxon snorted. "He doesn't scare me. Besides, there's no fighting fate." Stroking his hand across her hair, he smiled. "And some things are worth a little pain."

Especially when the reward is lots of pleasure.

* * * *

Vivid green eyes peered down at her, and she heard the most beautiful mulatto man she'd ever seen say, "And some things are worth a little pain."

Who is he, and what is he talking about? The man held her attention, and not just because of his mischievous smile, which widened the more he stared but because he made her want to do things—dirty things, like press her lips to his, lick her way along his cocoa skin, and nibble him.

Good God, what is wrong with me? It seemed her topsy-turvy turmoil hadn't ended. Along with this thought came the remembrance that the last thing she recalled, someone had accosted her in an alley as she attempted to escape Gavin.

Alarm made her eyes widen, and she scrambled to escape the lap she sat cuddled on.

"Easy, sweet cheeks. You're in good hands."

"More like groping ones," rumbled a familiar voice. Her gaze darted forward to see the giant from before.

Turning his head to the side, giving her his profile, one of his warm brown eyes met hers. "It's okay, Bailey. We took care of those rogues and got you out of there."

"But I didn't want to go," she argued in a little voice. It seemed, against her wishes, Gavin and Wyatt had gotten their way, and in retrospect, despite the uncertainty of the situation, she wasn't too sure if that wasn't the right choice. They'd not exaggerated, apparently, the danger she still found herself in a danger she didn't understand. She'd gone from no one wanting her to too many people wanting a piece. It made her head spin.

Having a muddled brain, though, didn't mean she didn't recognize the hard ridge poking at her backside. Worse, the stranger's erection didn't repulse her as it should have. Alarmed that her slutty ways appeared to be expanding to include all of Gavin's friend's, she pushed at the arms holding her.

"Let me go."

To her surprise, he complied, and she moved to the side, pressing herself against the passenger door, not recognizing the scenery flying by.

"Was Jaxon misbehaving?" Parker asked in a menacing tone.

She chewed her lip as she darted her gaze Jaxon's way. His eyes danced with mirth, and his lips quirked. "No more than usual," he replied.

A grunt sounded from the front seat. "You can sit up here with me if you'd like. I know how to keep my hands to myself."

Bailey didn't want to hurt Jaxon's feelings. However, she truly wanted to find out where they were going and maybe pump the seemingly friendly Parker for information. "Sorry. You didn't do a thing wrong, honestly," she claimed as she crawled through the middle console until she dropped into the front seat.

"No offense taken, sweet cheeks. If you change your mind, come on back, and we'll *cuddle*."

"Idiot." Parker's rumbled curse set the handsome Jaxon laughing.

A blush stained Bailey's cheeks, but she couldn't help the pleasure that swept her at Jaxon's blatant flirting. A girl always liked knowing a member of the opposite sex found her attractive.

But I doubt Gavin would like it. Shame suffused her as she realized Gavin would probably take issue with his friend so obviously hitting on her when he'd more or less staked her as his. That was if she considered the kiss he'd given her some kind of claim. She didn't even want to think about what the bite he'd given her meant. Although Wyatt hadn't found it strange in the least and had even encouraged it.

Some weird gang ritual perhaps? Raising her hand to her nape, she discovered a raised ridge that she'd bet would match one pair of cowboy teeth, but either she'd been passed out longer than expected or she'd once again spontaneously healed because not only did it not pain her but the skin, while bumpy as if scarred, didn't have a scabbed feel to it.

What's happening to me? Nothing in her life seemed normal anymore, from the abduction to her dramatic rescue to her second abduction by men who could model for *Playgirl*, to say nothing of her sudden X-Men ability to heal. *Is this all a very vivid dream? Or have I gone insane?*

"What's wrong?"

Parker's question took her from her musings, and she perused him as she struggled with something to say that didn't sound crazy.

"Where are you taking me? And don't you dare say somewhere safe because I am sick and tired of hearing that."

His lips twitched. "How about if I said we're going camping with rabid squirrels?"

A snort escaped her that turned into a short laugh. "That's your idea of telling me the truth?"

"Actually, he is," piped in Jaxon, who leaned forward with his arms braced behind her headrest. "On our trip up here, we stopped at some national park and put up some tents. We had a few beers, shot the shit, and went to bed. Well, in the middle of the night, something starts hitting our tents and making these really fucked-up noises. So, we all run out to see what the hell is going in, and we see, like, a dozen squirrels dive-bombing the tents. They no sooner bounced off them than they're running up a tree and jumping all over again."

"You're screwing with me," she replied, and when Jaxon used his fingers to cross his heart, she turned to Parker.

"For once, he's not exaggerating. Of course, the funniest part is when Wyatt starts freaking out, yelling at them, and does one of the little buggers not up and jump on his swinging dick."

She sucked in a horrified breath. "No! Oh my God, is he all right?" It seemed a shame if such a fine-looking man had lost his ability to, well, please a woman because of some freakish mishap with nature.

"He's fine. He heals fast just like you do. But, damn, the scream he let out when that squirrel dug its claws in . . . I doubt he'll ever live that down."

"So how did you get the squirrels to stop?"

"Tossed them some peanuts, of course."

Bailey couldn't help the laughter from bubbling up. "You guys are whacked. So with all that, you are intending to take me back there? Doesn't sound too safe to me."

"Don't worry, baby," Parker said with a smile tossed her way. "You can sleep with me. I'll keep you safe."

She couldn't believe he'd said it, nor the wink he gave her. "Um, I think Gavin might take issue with that."

"You might be surprised. The offer's there if you change your mind."

"And they say I'm the flirt of the group. Parker, my man, I am so proud of you. Hitting on the lady like that."

The growl the gentle giant sent Jaxon's way did nothing to deter him from his teasing. When Parker finally barked that if he didn't shut up, he'd pull the truck over and put Jaxon over his knee, silence finally reigned—if you ignored her stifled giggles because, truly, Jaxon was quite entertaining.

"Parker?"

"Yes, baby?"

"Why is this all happening to me? I mean, I went from being all alone, without even a BFF because she cheated on me with my boyfriend, to having your group and those other nasty guys all chasing me. Why? I'm not anyone special."

"I disagree with that. I think you are very special, and attractive. May I offer my fist so you can use it to knock out your obviously deranged ex-boyfriend?"

A wan smile curved her lips. "I don't blame him. I mean you don't know Becky. She's pretty and slim, and—"

"Obviously a shallow, insecure bitch if she saw nothing wrong with touching your man," Jaxon finished.

Turning in her seat, she fixed the mulatto hottie with her gaze. "And how is that different from you both flirting with me knowing Gavin's interested?"

"My mama taught me to share." The wicked grin he gave her said more than his words and painted a picture of naked bodies intertwined, sharing erotic delights. She bit her lip so as to not gasp.

"Where we come from," Parker interjected, "it is not uncommon for women to have more than one man in her life at the same time."

"Oh my God, are you guys like some Mormon cult then?" Her brow creased. "Wait, I thought they believed in multiple wives."

Jaxon whistled with amusement. "I can't wait to hear you explain your way out of this one, big guy."

"Um, well, you see . . ." Parker tapered off, his face alternately blushing and looking uncomfortable. "Can't we just wait until we meet up with Gavin and Wyatt? They'll probably explain it better."

"Explain what? That you guys belong to some freakish sex cult that shares their women? Count me out."

Bailey peered out the side window at the never-ending trail of trees. With her new ability to heal, could she jump and make it into the woods before they could stop and chase her?

"Don't you even think about leaving this truck."

"Or what? You and your buddy will tie me down and make me into your sex slave?"

"Ooh, count me in. That sounds like fun."

"Shut it, Jaxon," Parker growled, his hands turning white where he clutched the steering wheel. "We. Are. Not. A. Sex. Cult." He enunciated each word, and oddly enough, despite what she'd learned so far, she believed him. Not that she let him off the hook that easily, not with the pile of unanswered questions she had still left to ask.

"Then what are you?"

"We are pack."

"What is pack?"

"That's all I'm saying for now."

And it was. No matter what she said or asked, Parker wouldn't answer, keeping his eyes fixed to the road. When she turned to Jaxon instead, he drew a pinched finger and thumb across his mouth in a zipping motion then shrugged.

Disgruntled, and more confused than ever, she sat back with her arms crossed and a scowl on her face. She didn't know which was worse, knowing she'd been kidnapped by some guys who were looking for an orgy or the fact that she wanted to participate.

I am turning into a major slut.

Chapter Eight

"We should stop in town and buy her some things, seeing as how everything else of hers was destroyed."

Gavin's voice, after such a long period of introspective silence, jolted Wyatt. Especially since they'd spent the last few hours coasting along at a moderate speed, keeping an eye open for any vehicles that might be trailing after them.

"You can emasculate yourself all you want browsing through the underwear section at the local Walmart, but count me out."

"There's nothing wrong with buying a woman some underwear, especially when she's your mate," Gavin replied indignantly.

"Yeah, but she's not mine. So no way am I prancing around holding up tops and pants, going, 'Do you think she'd like this?'" Wyatt adopted a high-pitched tone that caused Gavin to let go of the steering wheel so he could launch a fist his way. Taking the blow with a grunt, Wyatt laughed. "You haven't even touched her pussy yet, and you're already whipped."

"Look who's talking," snorted Gavin. "You are trying so hard to bullshit that you don't give a damn

that your face is turning a deep shade of brown."

"Don't try and make up crap that doesn't exist," Wyatt snarled. "The girl might be your woman, but that doesn't make her mine."

"Liar. Keep fighting it then. I can't wait to see how you're going to cope when I make her cry out in pleasure tonight. Her sweet, hot flesh wrapped around my cock. Her—"

It was Gavin's turn to grunt as Wyatt smacked him back. "I am not going to be jealous. Or envious. Or anything because Bailey means nothing to me." Adamant words he spoke, and yet, Wyatt recognized them as false. "Let me off here."

"Here" was a deserted spot that marked the outer edge of the park, a few miles from town. Slowing down, Gavin put the SUV in park and gave him a hard look.

"I know you're in denial, but do me a favor and think long and hard about Bailey. About becoming her mate. If I have to share her with anyone, I'd really prefer it to be you."

"Assuming she'll even have me. You seem to forget she knows nothing of our ways. And with Nathan's new rules, it's her choice, despite what you did back at her place. Even if I did want to, I doubt she'll overcome her human upbringing enough to ever agree to it."

"So we show her why two men is better than one."

A rusty chuckle escaped him. "Damn, like those

Chapter Eight

"We should stop in town and buy her some things, seeing as how everything else of hers was destroyed."

Gavin's voice, after such a long period of introspective silence, jolted Wyatt. Especially since they'd spent the last few hours coasting along at a moderate speed, keeping an eye open for any vehicles that might be trailing after them.

"You can emasculate yourself all you want browsing through the underwear section at the local Walmart, but count me out."

"There's nothing wrong with buying a woman some underwear, especially when she's your mate," Gavin replied indignantly.

"Yeah, but she's not mine. So no way am I prancing around holding up tops and pants, going, 'Do you think she'd like this?'" Wyatt adopted a high-pitched tone that caused Gavin to let go of the steering wheel so he could launch a fist his way. Taking the blow with a grunt, Wyatt laughed. "You haven't even touched her pussy yet, and you're already whipped."

"Look who's talking," snorted Gavin. "You are trying so hard to bullshit that you don't give a damn

that your face is turning a deep shade of brown."

"Don't try and make up crap that doesn't exist," Wyatt snarled. "The girl might be your woman, but that doesn't make her mine."

"Liar. Keep fighting it then. I can't wait to see how you're going to cope when I make her cry out in pleasure tonight. Her sweet, hot flesh wrapped around my cock. Her—"

It was Gavin's turn to grunt as Wyatt smacked him back. "I am not going to be jealous. Or envious. Or anything because Bailey means nothing to me." Adamant words he spoke, and yet, Wyatt recognized them as false. "Let me off here."

"Here" was a deserted spot that marked the outer edge of the park, a few miles from town. Slowing down, Gavin put the SUV in park and gave him a hard look.

"I know you're in denial, but do me a favor and think long and hard about Bailey. About becoming her mate. If I have to share her with anyone, I'd really prefer it to be you."

"Assuming she'll even have me. You seem to forget she knows nothing of our ways. And with Nathan's new rules, it's her choice, despite what you did back at her place. Even if I did want to, I doubt she'll overcome her human upbringing enough to ever agree to it."

"So we show her why two men is better than one."

A rusty chuckle escaped him. "Damn, like those

Chapter Eight

"We should stop in town and buy her some things, seeing as how everything else of hers was destroyed."

Gavin's voice, after such a long period of introspective silence, jolted Wyatt. Especially since they'd spent the last few hours coasting along at a moderate speed, keeping an eye open for any vehicles that might be trailing after them.

"You can emasculate yourself all you want browsing through the underwear section at the local Walmart, but count me out."

"There's nothing wrong with buying a woman some underwear, especially when she's your mate," Gavin replied indignantly.

"Yeah, but she's not mine. So no way am I prancing around holding up tops and pants, going, 'Do you think she'd like this?'" Wyatt adopted a high-pitched tone that caused Gavin to let go of the steering wheel so he could launch a fist his way. Taking the blow with a grunt, Wyatt laughed. "You haven't even touched her pussy yet, and you're already whipped."

"Look who's talking," snorted Gavin. "You are trying so hard to bullshit that you don't give a damn

that your face is turning a deep shade of brown."

"Don't try and make up crap that doesn't exist," Wyatt snarled. "The girl might be your woman, but that doesn't make her mine."

"Liar. Keep fighting it then. I can't wait to see how you're going to cope when I make her cry out in pleasure tonight. Her sweet, hot flesh wrapped around my cock. Her—"

It was Gavin's turn to grunt as Wyatt smacked him back. "I am not going to be jealous. Or envious. Or anything because Bailey means nothing to me." Adamant words he spoke, and yet, Wyatt recognized them as false. "Let me off here."

"Here" was a deserted spot that marked the outer edge of the park, a few miles from town. Slowing down, Gavin put the SUV in park and gave him a hard look.

"I know you're in denial, but do me a favor and think long and hard about Bailey. About becoming her mate. If I have to share her with anyone, I'd really prefer it to be you."

"Assuming she'll even have me. You seem to forget she knows nothing of our ways. And with Nathan's new rules, it's her choice, despite what you did back at her place. Even if I did want to, I doubt she'll overcome her human upbringing enough to ever agree to it."

"So we show her why two men is better than one."

A rusty chuckle escaped him. "Damn, like those

girls we tag-teamed in college? Fuck. I'd almost forgotten about that." Again a lie. No man could ever forget the incredible erotic feeling of sharing a woman's body with another.

"Think about it while you're taking your run in the woods. And while I'd really prefer no interruptions tonight for our first time together, you are more than welcome anytime after that."

Wyatt didn't trust himself to reply, not with his mind suddenly full of images that made his cock stiffen. He swung out of the truck and stripped quickly in the shadows before he handed his clothes to his friend. After shifting first into his beast, a bone-melting and crunching transformation that, while painful, no longer made him scream, he tore off into the woods. He needed to run to clear his mind before he dealt with the female who roused a myriad of feelings in him that he didn't know how to deal with, that made him want things he'd never imagined.

Lust he could understand. She possessed a fine figure made for accepting a man's body and seed.

Protectiveness he could fathom as well because of her ordeal and her fragile nature. What male wouldn't want to step up and take over the role of hero? However, thoughts of forever and mating . . . what the fuck was that all about?

Wyatt understood the whole mating process. A male met a nice-smelling she-wolf, he bit her, and they settled down to have cubs, sometimes with another male, or more, joining the group. Or a male met a human female, he fucked her, and kept her to himself, living out his days working for the pack while watching others raise their cubs.

Then there was his situation. A human girl who wasn't, who'd attracted the attention, it seemed, of four males, and not just any males, two who could have been pack alphas. It made no sense. In the history passed down by their elders, he'd never heard of such a thing. And it drove him nuts that it had happened to him.

I have no need or interest in mating, an easy thing to pronounce to himself and Gavin, but much harder face-to-face with her, a dilemma made more difficult by the needs of his wolf. Even now, his inner beast paced inside, agitated that he hadn't marked the female and that they were dawdling in the woods instead of making their way instantly to her side to protect her.

Being forced wasn't something that sat well with Wyatt, especially not for something that would affect the rest of his life. *It's not as if I don't like her, and if I had to share with anyone, this group of men would be my first choice.* Well, maybe not the annoying Jaxon, but still, he could handle the pup. So what exactly bothered him the most about the concept of mating with Bailey?

Until he found out, he'd fight the urge tooth and nail and take cold showers. *Lots and lots of them*, he amended, because as soon as he reached the outskirts of the campground where Parker and Jaxon had already set up the tents, his wolf took over. Wyatt could only watch, a passenger in his own mind, as his more bestial side, scenting the female it wanted, bounded into the clearing they'd chosen to set up camp.

Of course, his wolf had forgotten one crucial fact. She didn't know what he and his pack brothers were. As soon as her eyes caught sight of him in his wolf form—a formidable beast, if he did say so himself—she scrambled up from the log she perched on and screamed loud enough to wake the dead. Before Parker or Jaxon could reach her, Wyatt changed back to his human shape, causing her to let loose with another formidable example of her lung capacity.

Slapping a hand over her mouth, he shushed her. It did nothing to calm her. She twisted but couldn't manage to escape his clutches. Caught, she made panicky sounds behind his hand that, for some reason, angered him.

As if I'd ever hurt her.

"Stop freaking out. It's me, Wyatt." That announcement did nothing to calm her. Actually, she struggled even more, and Wyatt tightened his grip. "Oh, for fuck's sake. Would you knock it off? I'm a Lycan. Big fucking deal. We all are, so the sooner you get over your hysterics, the quicker I get my hand off your mouth and we can discourse like grownups."

Ire flashed in her eyes, replacing her fear. Under the palm of his hand, he felt her jaw work as she struggled to open her mouth. She didn't manage to, not with the tight seal he'd created, but the motion and the situation suddenly caught up to him. It came to him that he stood very close to her, naked, and while his one hand kept her silent, his other had somehow curled around her waist to draw her into him. While his psyche might not have instantly noticed the awkward situation, his cock certainly did, rising and butting against her lower tummy.

Bite her. His wolf's demand came through loud and clear. *Ah shit.*

Wyatt jumped back from her, releasing her in his sudden need to escape. He glanced about, looking for Jaxon or Parker to help defuse the situation, but they'd melted into the woods, giving him some unwanted privacy.

At least she didn't immediately start shrieking, but she looked far from happy. "A Lycan. What the fuck is that?" she yelled, obscenity peppering her language and making Wyatt wince. Men cursed. Women, well, they just didn't, damn it.

"Can you take it down a notch? I'd rather not announce it to the whole fucking world."

"Or what? You'll maul me again? Go ahead. It's what you all seem to do best."

"Oh, cut the melodrama. We've never actually hurt you. On the contrary, everything we've done is to keep your ass safe." Wyatt kept his words blunt, lest he give in to the temptation to cross the space between them and fold her in his arms. He could see the tears brimming in her eyes despite her brave words and smell her fear. It roused every protective instinct he owned, plus some he'd never known.

"Safe! You all keep saying that like it answers everything. Well, I've got news for you. It doesn't. I am not some goddamned object you can just pick up and carry around. I am a person. Don't you get that?"

"Yup, a person who's in danger, so stop your whining." He intentionally goaded her, anything to wipe the terrified scent from her. Surely getting her riled up was better than letting her stew in fear.

It worked. Her jaw dropped. "Whining? Screw you. I am so sick and tired of all the bullshit and lies. I've had it. I am not doing anything or going anywhere else until someone gives me some answers." She planted her hands on her hips in a belligerent stance.

Face to face with her wrath, Wyatt found himself utterly enchanted. Her eyes flashed, her cheeks bloomed, and her chest heaved. Hot damn, did his wolf fight for control, wanting to mark the feisty female who'd managed to upset his carefully balanced world—a woman he wanted to suddenly claim as his own with a ferocity that shocked him.

Not without a fight I'm not. He couldn't claim her if she didn't want him.

"Were your ears not working earlier? I told you

the truth when I said we're Lycan. As in werewolves. You know, men who turn into wolves." He flashed some teeth at her.

Uncertainty crossed her face. "Impossible."

He snorted. "Really? 'Cause just a second ago you were screaming mighty hard for someone who didn't believe her own eyes."

"It's the stress of it all. I must have imagined it."

"Imagined a massive wolf turning into a man? If that's the case, how come I know exactly what you saw?"

"I've heard of hallucinations being contagious. Some kind of crowd effect."

"Think again, sunshine. It was real, and you know it."

"Oh yeah? Then show me again."

"Why the fuck would I do that? My ears are still ringing from the last time."

Crossing her arms over her chest, she tapped her foot. "Listen here, asshole. In the last little while, I've been kidnapped, drugged, almost raped, attacked by wolves, rescued and then kidnapped again, attacked, and brought to some faraway woods with killer squirrels by a perverted sex cult who thinks they're werewolves. I think I deserve a little understanding, so would it kill you to fucking show me your furry dog again?" She ended her speech on a holler.

"Are you on your period or something?" he replied. "'Cause you're awfully crabby."

"Oooh!" Her inarticulate cry of rage went well with her swinging fists and charge that took her right into his body. Not that she did any damage. He caught her flailing wrists and yanked her arms above her head, pulling her taut against his body.

"Enough of the temper tantrums, sunshine. I am a Lycan. Accept it, and no, I am not changing my skin like some trained circus animal to prove it again." Besides, he didn't trust his wolf to not take what it wanted, mainly Bailey.

"Nothing makes sense anymore."

"I don't like this situation any better than you. You think I want to babysit some human girl who's not a wolf?"

"Then let me go."

He shook his head. "No can do. You're a part of this group now whether you like it or not. Gavin made sure of that when he marked you."

"That's the second time you've said that. What the hell are you talking about?"

"Remember when you bit each other?"

She nodded her head.

"With Lycans that's the same as marriage."

"What!" Her eyes just about fell out of her head. "I never agreed to that."

"Doesn't matter. The blood bond has been formed between you and Gavin. It's unbreakable." He didn't mention that death could sever it. She might take that as an invitation to go on a murderous spree.

"I don't believe you."

"Believe it, sunshine. And be careful, you're making my wolf really agitated. I'd hate to accidentally bite you too. I doubt either of us would like that."

"You mean, be married to two of you?" Her voice dropped to a whisper. "Parker said something about that, but that's crazy. I mean normal people don't marry multiple people."

"But we're not normal." He drew her closer as he said this, his gaze locked to hers. Her body trembled, and he couldn't stop himself from touching his lips to hers. A touch he hadn't meant, but once started, he couldn't stop. He took what she so innocently offered, tasted the sweetness of her mouth, and wanted more.

The crackling sound of underbrush as several someones approached camp in an obvious fashion made him release her and stumble back as if burned.

Not burned enough, though, according to his throbbing cock. It screamed at him to finish what he'd started, a need forgotten when Gavin stepped from the woods flanked by Jaxon and Parker, who helped him carry some boxes.

"Did you marry me when you bit me?" she blurted out upon seeing Gavin.

Looking startled, Gavin hesitated. "Um, kind of."

"I want a divorce!" Bailey yelled. "You—you jerk."

"No," was his flat reply. Stormy blue eyes met

Wyatt's. "What the fuck happened while I was gone?" he snarled.

"Mr. Calm and Collected accidentally strode into camp wearing his wolf," Jaxon announced, earning himself a throttling for later.

"Then he shifted to try and calm her," Parker added.

"And that's when I found out we're supposedly married. I didn't agree to that, so you annul whatever you did, cowboy, right now!" Bailey practically spat she was so livid.

Wyatt didn't envy Gavin's duty of calming her down and refused to feel guilt over having caused the current turmoil. *She would have found out sooner or later. No time like the present, I always say.*

"Oh, bloody hell." Dropping the box he held, Gavin strode toward Bailey and upended her over his shoulder, to which she predictably freaked, screeching and pounding at his back.

Wyatt turned from the spectacle, not out of embarrassment but more because he found her squirming antics much too interesting. Apparently, though, his torture was to continue.

"Wyatt!" Gavin barked. "Tent. Now."

Throwing a scowl at the smirking Jaxon, and a snarl at Parker, he stalked after his pack brother— and the woman his wolf wanted to claim as mate. Worse, so did the man.

* * * *

Bailey didn't recall ever being this angry before. Or scared.

When the wolf strode from the woods, she'd thought she'd piss her pants. When the wolf, in some screwed-up body-molting process, turned into Wyatt, she did lose a few drops.

Here I thought I'd come to grips with the fact I was abducted by a cult who wanted to have sex with me. Heck, I was even thinking I might enjoy it. Then Wyatt dropped a werewolf bomb followed by a marriage one, and she no longer knew if the earth rotated around the sun or if she'd somehow ended up in an alternate universe because in her world, shit like this just didn't happen.

She did the only thing she could think of when faced with facts her mind refused to believe. She freaked. Of course, her temper tantrum had the interesting result of getting Wyatt to manhandle her first, followed by Gavin.

The whole situation was enough to drive a girl batty. And horny.

Only once he thrust her into a tent, which Parker had erected before all hell broke loose, did Gavin release her, and she scurried to the farthest corner. She crouched in a defensive posture, suspicious of the two men who sat on their haunches before her. They really were distracting, Gavin with his blond cowboy good looks and Wyatt because he was pretty bloody naked. Never mind the fact that he was built like a god.

Seriously. She might currently seesaw between mad and terrified, but she couldn't help but notice Wyatt's toned musculature and his tanned skin, which stretched all over his sculpted frame. Then, there was his cock.

Her eyes drew down to that shadowy vee between his legs, and the blush in her cheeks mounted as she saw movement.

A soft growl broke the silence. "I shouldn't be here," Wyatt said. "This is between you and your mate."

"Too bad. As my second, I am ordering you to stay. You helped cause the situation. You can help me fix it."

She hated the way they kept talking as if she wasn't there. "The only way this is getting fixed is if you let me go."

Brilliant blue eyes that still took her breath away, even given the crazy things she now knew, met hers. "You are mine, darling. Where you go, I go. Better get used to it."

"What if I don't want to?"

"You don't really have a choice. I marked you."

For some reason, his answer irritated her. It sounded so clinical. "Wyatt says it's like a marriage thing for werewolves."

"It is. We call it claiming our mate."

"But can't it still be broken? I mean we didn't have sex or anything yet."

"Don't worry. I plan to rectify that problem shortly."

Gavin stood up in the full-sized tent and began to unbutton his shirt.

Her mouth went dry as the pale skin of his chest emerged. "Um, what are you doing?"

"You seem a little put out that we haven't consummated our joining, darling. I'm just trying to do my husbandly duty."

"But-But . . ." She lost her train of thought as the shirt went flying, displaying a lean physique. His hands went to the buckle on his jeans. Despite herself, she couldn't prevent a burgeoning of heat from forming in her lower tummy.

"I don't believe it, Gavin. You've rendered her speechless." Wyatt, still sitting on his heels, regarded her with dark eyes and a partial sneer.

She licked her lips, moistening them so she could speak. "What if I don't want to have sex?"

"Oh, you will," Gavin assured her. She averted her eyes as he slid his pants down, the heat in her cheeks—and cleft—rising with his husky chuckle.

"But we're not alone."

"Better get used to it, darling. In the pack, the women take multiple mates, and many enjoy them at the same time."

Oh, that was a definite quiver in her cleft at his words but also trepidation. "I'm not pack, as you call it, and Wyatt's not my mate."

"Not yet, but he will be soon, maybe even before

the end of the night. Won't you, Wyatt?"

Her eyes rose to meet Wyatt's, and the intense expression sucked the breath from her. She'd never seen such hunger on a man's face before, but she recognized it. Worse, she wanted it.

"I never agreed to any of this. I'll hate you if you force me." She made the mistake of looking up and caught Gavin's full nude body. She let out a small cry, not of distress but desire. A blond god stood before her, the evidence of his arousal jutting forth, the burning desire in Wyatt's gaze repeated on Gavin's face.

"Come here, darling. Come and kiss me. If you can kiss me and then still tell me you don't want me, I will let you walk away."

"I don't believe you."

"I am a man of my word."

"He is," Wyatt added. "We all are."

Oddly, she believed them. "So, one kiss, and if I say no, you'll let me go."

"Yes."

"Promise me."

Gavin rolled his eyes. "I promise. Now come here."

Her eyes flicked to Wyatt, but he said not a word, nor did he look away. Almost as if her feet belonged to someone else, she stepped forward. It took only a few paces to bring her within reach, and even before Gavin touched her, she knew she was in trouble because her whole body burned to feel his touch. It frightened her, and she took a half-step back.

"I won't hurt you," Gavin whispered. "I would never hurt you, my mate."

He held his hands out, palms upward, waiting. She chewed her lip as she looked into his eyes. *I don't have a choice. I can't escape. I have to kiss him.* The problem was, she knew once she did, she'd never say no.

And why should I? Here was a man who wanted her, a man who was something more, who'd done everything since meeting her to keep her safe and to show his interest. Why did she keep acting as if he was the enemy? *Because he might eat me?*

As quickly as the thought hit, she discarded it. Gavin wouldn't harm her, but he would give her pleasure. She didn't know yet how she felt about the whole mated-for-life thing. Shouldn't love be the deciding factor? But mate or not, as well as love or not, she couldn't deny desire. Perhaps if she quenched the thirst of her body, and his, she'd find the strength to walk away, and his lust assuaged, maybe he'd let her go.

All those thoughts took only a moment, a slim sliver of time, as Gavin patiently waited, hands outstretched.

She slipped her fingers into the open palms, and he curled his digits around hers, reeling her in slowly, his eyes locked with hers.

She tilted her head back and didn't flutter her eyes closed until his lips brushed hers. A soft sigh escaped her lips at the sense of rightness his touch engendered, a feeling of coming home, and in that moment, she knew, one time, two times, a million embraces like this could happen, and she'd never want to leave—would never tire of his kiss.

Looks like I've got myself a mate.

And like any new wife, no matter the method of her claiming, she wanted a wedding night. As he deepened his kiss, his tongue venturing forth to toy at the seam of her lips, she twined her arms around his neck, showing her willingness. Parting her lips, she met his oral thrust, the taste of him, peppermint and *man,* sending tingles throughout her body, right down to her toes.

It barely registered when hands lowered her to an air mattress, Gavin's body partially splayed across hers. Deft fingers tugged her shirt off, breaking the embrace only long enough to skim the top over her head. Her upper body unclothed, she received the full impact of Gavin's skin against hers. It made her moan, especially when he rubbed his scorching flesh against hers, abrading her nipples, which thrust up eagerly, demanding some attention.

As if sensing their silent plea, his mouth left hers, trailing light kisses along her jaw, down her neck, and to the valley between her breasts. She clutched at his head, her fingers twining in his silken strands as he rubbed the rough edge of his jaw against her tender skin.

"Gavin, please."

He chuckled softly against her skin before making her gasp as he finally grasped one of her turgid nipples in his mouth, his hard suction sending her bucking up off the mattress.

He planted his body more firmly over her, his upper arms holding him up off her torso while his lower body pinned her, the hotness of his cock nudging at her still-clothed cleft. It drove her wild, and she squirmed under him, wanting . . . yearning . . . needing him inside her.

When he dragged his mouth to her other neglected areola, she cried out, her cleft tightening as he tortured her bud. She couldn't take the pleasure. It was too intense. She tugged at his head, trying to draw him back up to kiss her.

A new set of hands grasped hers and pulled them above her head, and her eyes flew open to see Wyatt kneeling behind her head, staring down at her, heated hunger in his eyes.

It should have freaked her out to have to him there, or embarrassed her at the very least. Instead, she trembled. "Please," she begged, not even sure what she asked for.

His lips swooped down to touch hers in a scorching embrace that, combined with Gavin's enthusiastic sucking, made her pussy tighten and quiver in a mini orgasm.

She clutched tightly at Wyatt's hands when Gavin began blazing a path down her stomach to the waistband of her pants. She moaned against his mouth when her bottoms went sliding down, exposing her.

A knuckle brushed across her clit and moist slit. She bucked, already so sensitive and primed for his touch. Gavin nestled himself between her parted thighs, the head of his cock nudging. She mewled in need, Wyatt's mouth swallowing the sound. Gyrating her hips, she begged without words, but Gavin didn't give her what she wanted.

Wyatt moved away, releasing her hands and lips, and she opened her eyes to find Gavin hovering over her.

"Do you still want to say no?" he asked, somehow managing to rub the head of his dick across her clit.

She sucked in breath. "You know I don't."

"Tell me. I want no excuses later."

She twined her arms around his neck and drew his unresisting body down until his lips hovered just above hers. "Take me. Please."

With a groan, he took her lips as his cock plowed into her cleft, sinking to the hilt. She started coming apart at the seams, her whole body shaking and at the same time coiling tightly against him. With his second and third thrusts, she came with a scream, her pussy rippling in blissful waves that made him moan against her mouth and pump even more frantically until, with a yell, he rocketed into her and went still, the hotness of his seed bathing her womb.

Gavin collapsed beside her but took her with

him, nestling her into his side. She opened her eyes and peeked around, discovering Wyatt gone. Surely it wasn't a pang of disappointment that went through her at the discovery?

She didn't have time to examine her surprising reaction because Gavin spoke. "I'm sorry that was so quick and rough. Next time, I'll take things slower and really give you pleasure."

Her mouth rounded in an O of surprise. "You mean it gets better?" He'd already given her the most powerful orgasm ever. Surely he jested.

"You ain't seen nothing yet, darling," he drawled.

"You are, of course, assuming there will be a second time," she impishly replied. "Just because we've had sex doesn't mean I don't still want some answers."

"I know, and I will give them to you. Keep in mind I didn't keep things from you out of maliciousness. It's just things moved so fast, and given our nature, we needed to be secretive. Everything might seem kind of scary right now, and you might resent me a bit for acting so high-handed, but I have to admit, I don't regret meeting and claiming you."

"Doesn't it frighten you, though?"

"What part? The rogues that are after you?"

"No, although they are pretty scary. I mean where you keep talking about it in terms of forever. You barely know me. What if you don't like me?"

"Fate wouldn't be so cruel." He chuckled,

brushing a kiss across her temple.

A thought occurred to her, two actually, and she scrambled upright to ask the first. "Hey, wait a second. You bit me, so since you're a werewolf, does that mean I'm going to go furry on the next full moon?" The idea both fascinated and repulsed her.

A grin stretched his face, displaying his gleaming white teeth. "Sorry. But lycanthropy is something we're born with."

"Oh. So I don't need to invest in a flea collar?"

"Nah, those critters tend to stay away from our kind. But mosquitoes, however, love us."

She smiled at his attempted humor, but she couldn't wait to ask her second question. "What about babies and, you know, STDs? I, um, kind of noticed you forgot to put a condom on."

"First off, we don't carry disease, nor can we catch any, so you're perfectly safe." A shadow fell over his eyes.

"And about the whole pregnancy thing. Humans and Lycans can't procreate. Something about our different genetic makeup makes it impossible."

"So, we'll never have children?" She'd never thought about it much before, but she'd kind of always assumed she'd have the expected pair, a boy and girl, to be exact. To suddenly discover, on top of everything else, that she'd never conceive saddened her.

As if sensing her moroseness, he hugged her tight. "I know it's a lot to take in, but I promise you, living with the pack will help."

"So is that the next stop in our trip? Home to your pack?" *Am I ready for that?*

"Almost. We'll need to drive tomorrow and make one more stop before finishing the trek back to our home."

"And then what?"

"Then, we start our life together."

A life doing what exactly, though? she wondered.

His kiss drove away her further questions, and by the time they were done with their languorous second round—where he kept his word and showed her even more rapturous heights—she was too tired to put words together coherently.

And she wasn't sure if she imagined or not his softly whispered, "Love you, darling. My mate, my heart."

* * * *

When Wyatt left the tent, he didn't initially go far because, for some reason, he just couldn't tear his eyes from the gyrating couple. He wanted to join in so badly—wanted to touch Bailey's silky skin, taste her sweet lips again, and sink his teeth into her flesh and irrevocably mark her.

With a grunt that sounded more animal than man, he ran from the campground, shifting into his wolf even before he hit the tree line. *Run away. Run from the temptation. Run from the future I did not choose.*

He howled as he bolted through the trees on four feet, his inner turmoil of earlier nothing compared to his current state. Now, he'd gotten a glimpse of her responsive nature, heard her mewling cries of pleasure, tasted her, and seen the ecstasy on his pack brother's face, a pleasure he could have if he weren't so scared to take it.

But was he ready for that kind of commitment? Ready to give himself over to a virtual stranger? To someone who knew nothing about his kind, his world?

Gavin seemed to have no qualms about that, and he'd bet Parker and Jaxon wouldn't either. However, Wyatt expected more, even if he didn't understand what that "more" was. It struck him that it wasn't the fact of her humanity, or other status, that bothered him. Nor did the sharing of her bother him, not when he could already imagine the bliss of it. What truly disturbed him about Bailey was the loss of control. For a man who prided himself on doing the right thing, no matter what, who always thought through his every move, his wild urge to bind himself without a thought for tomorrow, without a care for compatibility because of an animalistic need, scared him.

I want more than just hormones to tie us. I want . . . love. The answer surprised him. He'd never thought himself the romantic type, but now that he'd recognized it, he couldn't deny it. He wanted a mating based on true affection.

Did Gavin already love Bailey? Had his friend found and embraced that elusive emotion? It seemed too soon, and yet, he couldn't deny Gavin's erratic behavior since he'd met Bailey. He also couldn't ignore his friend's unstoppable need to find her when she went missing and to keep her safe once he had. *Feelings I now share.*

It occurred to Wyatt, as his wild dash through the woods slowed, that he'd never before felt this way about a woman, never actually thought twice about one. Analyzing his emotions, he recognized he admired Bailey's spirit, especially given the circumstances she'd recently gone through. He liked that she questioned them and didn't take at face value what they told her. She possessed a mind of her own. Unlike she-wolves, Bailey didn't just roll over and show her belly because a male said to. She displayed courage even in the face of fear and the unknown. It occurred to him just how brave she had to be to stand up to him even after discovering he could shift into a wolf. He alone outweighed her by probably by at least sixty pounds of muscle, yet she'd demanded—looking adorably delicious—that he and Gavin let her go.

Slumping into a heap of leaves, Wyatt chuffed into the decaying foliage. *Fuck me to hell and back. Short acquaintance or not, I think I might love her.*

The knowledge didn't lessen his mental burden. *Because, now that I know, I won't accept anything less from her.* In other words, he couldn't just claim her and seduce her into caring like Gavin had. No, as with all things in his life, Wyatt would do it the hard way. He'd wait for her to come to the realization she loved him on her own.

I just hope she does it quickly, or my blue balls are liable to fall off.

Chapter Nine

Bailey woke, spooned into Gavin's body. It seemed her new werewolf husband was very happy to see her if the cock rubbing against her backside was any indication. His lips brushed the skin below her ear, sending a shiver through her.

"Morning, darling."

"Hi." A trite reply but all she could manage as she suddenly found herself tongue-tied in the light of day. It was one thing to give herself to passion without any abandon the night before, another to realize the man whose arms cradled her thought he owned her—and planned to share her with his buddies.

Except for Wyatt. He couldn't get out of here fast enough last night, she recalled, the realization oddly saddening. *He must not have liked what he saw.* Her curves weren't for everyone. *Look at me getting morose over the fact I have to satisfy myself with only one lover.* Bailey wanted to slap herself for being so stupid.

Besides, how could she feel unattractive with Gavin's calloused fingers stroking over her nipples, tightening them into points. Moisture flooded her cleft, and she sighed as she wiggled against him. Despite the questions and trepidation over the future clouding her mind, she couldn't deny she enjoyed parts of the life she found herself thrust into. *One large part especially,* she thought with a grin.

"Hey, you lovebirds want some breakfast?" Jaxon broke the erotic spell as he stuck his head into the tent opening, and Gavin groaned.

"Your timing sucks."

"No, it doesn't, judging by your tone." Jaxon grinned unrepentantly and winked at Bailey. "You hungry, sweet cheeks? Sounds like you might have worked up quite the appetite last night."

Bailey buried her face against Gavin's arms, her cheeks warm, as his body shook with either repressed laughter or anger. She couldn't tell.

A meaty smack sounded from outside the tent, along with a terse, "Watch your mouth, puppy," that had Jaxon backing out.

Wyatt! She tamped down her excitement with the reminder that, despite his hungry kisses the day before, he wanted no part of her and the love triangle Gavin proposed.

As if reading some of her thoughts, Gavin whispered, "Don't worry, darling. He'll come around. Even he can't fight fate."

Fate has nothing to do with it. She didn't reply because she worried that if she protested she didn't want him, Wyatt might hear, and if she did show an interest, she might hurt Gavin's feelings.

Damn. Having more than one guy in my life is complicated. She couldn't even imagine more than that. As she crawled off the squishy air mattress, a box preceded Wyatt as he entered the tent. With a squeak, she dove for the bed and the concealing blanket.

Gavin laughed. "Darling, I think he's already seen the parts you're trying to hide."

"Let her have her modesty," Wyatt gruffly said, not meeting her eyes, which peeked over the sheet, reinforcing Bailey's belief that he preferred her covered up.

Apparently, modesty wasn't a werewolf trait because a very naked Gavin stretched as he stood, his body a work of art that made her almost slobber. And to think he'd chosen her as his mate. It boggled the mind but delighted her body.

Gavin caught her rapt gaze, and his lips curved into a slow, sensual grin. "I'm going to find some coffee. Want some, darling?"

"Yes, please. With sugar and milk if possible."

The view of Gavin's taut buttocks as he strode from the tent proved quite enjoyable. She expected Wyatt to follow, but instead, he delved through the box and began pulling out articles of clothing.

"Gavin bought you some stuff while he was in town yesterday. He had to guess on the sizes, though, so don't kill him if he got it wrong." Wyatt handed her the clothes, which meant she had to let go of the sheet with one hand.

Mirth made his lips tilt. "You don't need to hide from me, sunshine. As Gavin mentioned, I've seen it all before."

"And left." She blurted the words out and immediately wanted the ground to open up and swallow her. "I . . . uh . . . that is . . . I mean, I understand. I mean, either you're not into that sharing thing like Gavin is claiming, or I wasn't to your taste. Totally cool."

Wyatt scowled. "You thought I left because of your looks?"

"Or because you aren't into the sharing thing," she reiterated defensively.

Before she could say boo, he'd dragged her from her nest of blankets onto his lap. She squealed and squirmed, trying to escape while her cheeks burned bright. However, his implacable grip didn't let her move.

"I think you look just fine, sunshine. Make that better than fine." He grasped her hand and placed it over his groin. "Feel that?"

How could she miss the throbbing cock in his pants? She nodded her head, unable to look him in the eye, especially since his blatant arousal brought a warmth to her cleft. *I don't understand how I can want him after just spending the night climaxing at the hands of his best friend.*

"Does that feel like a man who doesn't like what he sees?"

"No. Then why did you leave?" she asked softly.

"Because, and this is going to sound stupid and I'll deny it if you repeat, I want you to choose me as your mate because you want me. Not because you're horny, or because someone tells you to, or because you want to make Gavin happy. I want you to want me, for me." As if his honest words embarrassed him, a ruddy color flooded his face.

Tilting her head back, she stared into his serious dark eyes. "And what if I do want you, for you?"

"Then I will make love to you for the rest of your life." He sealed his promise with a sensual kiss that made her yearn for more, but a, "Hey, you guys mind waiting to do the naughty tango until tonight? Gavin says we need to get going," broke them apart.

Panting slightly, she stared at Wyatt, who grinned ruefully as he stroked her cheek. "And people wonder why I want to kill him."

Bailey laughed along with him but couldn't erase the burning touch of his kiss. It flattered her to know he wanted her, but she loved even more that he wanted her to make the decision and that he wanted more than just lust to draw them together. It made her fall in love with a second man. *I am so going to burn in hell for this.*

* * * *

Bailey ended up riding with Jaxon and Parker again as Gavin and Wyatt cleaned up their camp and checked for signs of pursuit. With Jaxon driving—to keep him out of trouble, Parker had explained with a grin—she ended up seated in the back with the giant.

Perfect, because she brimmed with questions, and now that the wolf was out of the bag, so to speak, she hoped he'd answer them.

"What's a pack?"

Parker's brows lifted. "Jumping right into it, are you? Fair enough. I guess there's no hiding anymore what we are. A pack is what we call a group of Lycans who live together under the rule of an alpha."

"So, what, you share a house, and one guy makes up the rules?"

A chuckle rumbled forth. "Not quite, baby. We tend to live on compounds, fairly self-sufficient ones, where we use solar energy and wind to create electricity, draw our water from wells, and where each family has its own house."

"Like the Amish," she supplied, trying to picture in her mind what exactly she'd encounter.

"Not quite as archaic. The men also work outside of the compound, their jobs providing the things we can't create on our own, such as packaged food, clothing, building materials, vehicles. We also maintain an account with a local butcher. We've discovered over the years that raising livestock around young'uns that aren't quite in control of their beast isn't a great idea."

"Eeew!" She scrunched up her nose at the picture his words painted. "So, the children are all wolves from birth?"

"Actually the Lycan gene manifests itself most often at puberty, usually on a full moon. It's considered a time of passage from childhood into adult and is celebrated by the whole pack."

Something he said caught her attention. "What do you mean most often?"

"Some of the children born of Lycan parents end up dormant. In other words, their wolf side doesn't ever emerge."

"What happens to them?"

Parker rolled his shoulders into a shrug. "Some stay and end up mating with a male who doesn't care if they have children or not because dormants and Lycans can't reproduce. Kind of like humans and us. Others leave the pack and settle among the humans, marrying them and having children."

"Do their children ever have the gene that makes them go furry?"

A shake of his head answered her.

"So how do you keep your population from dying out? I mean, it seems to me that it must be hard to maintain any kind of growth with that working against you."

"That's where multiple mates come in," Parker said with a grin. "It was discovered a long time ago that the ratio of females able to bear cubs versus males was low. We're talking four to six males for every she-wolf. Because diversity is required for any healthy population, the council leaders at the time created the pack laws. One of those laws states female Lycans must take a minimum of two mates or, even better, to ease the stress on the packs, up to four."

"That's barbaric!" she exclaimed. "You mean the women don't have a choice?"

Parker squirmed as if uncomfortable. "In the past they didn't, but things are slowly changing. One of the things Nathan did when he was placed in charge of the council was to modify the law to at least allow the females to choose for themselves, as opposed to the past, when the pack alpha or the father would choose for her with no regard for her feelings in the matter."

A frown creased her brow. "Still, you're talking about forcing women to be part of an orgy whether they want to or not."

A snort from the front of the vehicle made her look forward, and she caught Jaxon's humorous gaze in the rearview mirror. "First off, don't knock a ménage until you've tried it, sweet cheeks. It's a whole bunch of fun for everyone. And second, while some matings do participate in group sex, others prefer the one-on-one approach. Heck, they even schedule it so that no one feels shafted."

"Speaking from experience, are you?" she asked, trying to quell an odd sense of jealousy that made no sense. Jaxon didn't belong to her. Why should she care what he did with his dick?

He chuckled, a knowing sound that made her blush. "I'm not mated, so no firsthand knowledge, just thirdhand. But I am game to try either scenario if it means I get to be with you."

How to respond to his blatant declaration? Her cleft seemed to scream yes, but suddenly shy and embarrassed at the unexpected direction of the conversation, she blushed brighter and bit her lip.

"Ease off, Jaxon. Poor Bailey here's still going through a bit of culture shock. Besides, I think we both know who's next in line to claim her."

Why did everyone assume she was going to get with Wyatt? He'd said the choice was up to her, and she hadn't actually made that decision yet. *But you probably will the next time you lay your lips on him*, her mind snickered, not at all fooled.

"How do you handle it?" she blurted out.

"Handle what?" Parker asked, his fingers toying with a strand of her hair.

"I mean, don't you get jealous? When I found out my ex-boyfriend was fucking my best friend behind my back while, at the same time, still doing me, I was crushed. Then pissed. It hurt, and I felt so betrayed. How can you guys stand it?"

"I'm good at sharing," Jaxon replied in a humorous tone.

"We all are for the most part," Parker amended. "Don't forget, we're taught from birth that we're going to share any mate we gain later on in life. We also have the examples of our parents, too, which makes this choice easier. Sure, there are some jealousies and, in some cases, wolves who can't handle it. But they tend to be rare or resolved in a way that leaves the female out of it. No matter the differences between males in a mated group, the first and foremost concern is keeping their woman happy."

"Wow, this is all so messed up. I mean, you hear about it happening, guys and girls hooking up with more than one person. Watching the reality shows is one thing, but the thought of it happening to me." She shook her head. "It seems impossible. I don't know if I'm ready for that. It sounds like a lot of work." Much of it erotic, and yet, it was hard enough to balance one boyfriend, let alone four.

"Take your time, baby. No one's saying you have to choose another three mates today. This is something that will affect the rest of your life. It's not something that should be done or taken lightly."

A boldness took her, and she looked Parker in the eye. "You wouldn't be offended if you had to wait?"

The smile he sent her way made her body much too warm. "Baby, just the fact you're contemplating choosing me makes the wait more than worth it."

"Oh, gag me with a spoon," Jaxon added. "What he means to say, and this goes for me too, is we'll wait, but we hope our poor throbbing dicks don't fall off while you get over your human principles and decide four men in bed is better than one."

Bailey's laughter rang out as Parker dove over the front seat, growling something about emasculating the pup. Parker let Jaxon live—unharmed—but did take over driving, forcing Jaxon to remain in the front, where he could keep an eye on him. Their intriguing conversation, though, did not resume, not that it mattered. Parker had given her lots of food for thought, and as they continued their drive, the banter lighter with Jaxon craned backward, regaling her with pack tales as Parker drove, she digested what she'd learned.

Can I handle having more than one man? She'd already pretty much decided she wanted Wyatt. She just didn't know if it was too soon with Gavin to say something. As for Parker and Jaxon . . . with Parker there wasn't any of the tumultuous fire she felt with Gavin and Wyatt, yet he drew her. He had a solid presence about him that comforted her. And she loved the way he spoke with her, and how he took his time to explain and didn't pressure her. She could easily fall for a guy like that.

Then there was Jaxon. While he drove the others nuts, he provided a much-needed comic relief to their more serious demeanors. He quite honestly cracked her up, and while his timing wasn't always the best, she truly enjoyed that about him. It didn't hurt that he looked like yummy chocolate candy too. She couldn't deny her attraction to him, and her intrigue at his repeated hints at a fivesome. Was such a combination even possible?

And would Wyatt or Gavin allow it?

Oh my God, what is happening with me? A few days ago,

I'd never have even contemplated taking more than one man at a time to bed, and now I'm planning on four. The realization shook her. It seemed as if they'd placed her under a spell that lowered her morals and made her want to do things, taboo things. As if a veil lifted from her eyes, she resolved to slow things down. There was no need to be hasty. After all, she had Gavin to satisfy her needs. If these men truly wanted her, they could wait as she settled into her new life and decided if she wanted to keep it.

Chapter Ten

"Something's changed about you," Gavin said to Wyatt a few hours into their journey. Up to that point, they'd carefully watched for signs of pursuit and called in a report to Nathan. According to their leader, the rogue incidences seemed to have stopped for the moment, but it wasn't news Gavin or his pack brother celebrated, not when it coincided with their rescue of Bailey.

Could Roderick have banded all the rogues and set them on our trail?

It made his blood run cold to even think it. He kept in regular contact with Parker, ahead of them with his precious mate, but he wouldn't breathe easy until they'd caught up.

"What makes you think anything's different?" Wyatt asked, turning to face him.

"You seem more relaxed for one, and you've stopped making smart-ass remarks about my mate."

A smile ghosted over his friend's lips. "Let's just say I think I might have found what's been missing in my life."

"For real? So you admit she's your mate too." A touch of chagrin touched him that he wouldn't get Bailey to himself for much longer, but the gladness that knowing his best friend would end up as part of his mating group more than compensated for it.

"Yes, but I'm content to wait until she's ready to accept me."

"Okay, who the hell are you, and what have you done with my best friend? Seriously, man, since when are you so Zen-like?"

"Since I met the right woman and realized a few truths about myself. Now shut up before I make you eat my fist."

"That's more like it," Gavin said, laughing. "On another note, what are we going to do about the full moon tonight?" While adult Lycans could control their beast side on full moons, it didn't mean they didn't crave, and need, to run wild under its luminous glow.

"We'll have to take turns, I guess."

Gavin frowned. "So, what, one of us goes for a run at a time?"

"Or a pair. If we don't go far, then we'll be close if something were to happen."

"Okay, then if we go with that scenario, then we'll let Jaxon go for a run first since he's the youngest and will have the hardest time fighting the impulse to shift. We'll send Parker with him. Once he's blown off a bit of steam, you and I will let our wolves out and run in widening circles around the camp, keeping an eye out for rogues until it's time to swap places again."

"You don't think we've lost them?"

"Ever get the feeling that danger is lurking just out of sight? My gut is telling me they're out there, just waiting for their moment to swoop in. And what better time than the full moon when our beasts are at their strongest and most distracted?"

"I won't argue with your gut instinct. It's saved our asses more than once. So, we'll take turns running with the moon and patrolling. What about Bailey?"

"What about her?"

"She was asking me yesterday to shift in front of her. I refused, not wanting her to start shrieking again, but . . ." Wyatt paused, and concern creased his face. "Are we gonna let her see us in all our glory, or are we doing it out of sight so as to not freak her?"

Lucky for him, Gavin had spent time pondering this question, so he had a ready answer. "The sooner she gets used to it, the better. We'll be in the compound by tomorrow afternoon. Better she gets over her shock now, in private, with us, than with the whole pack."

"Good point."

After that, they lapsed into silence again, although Gavin's thoughts were anything but. Yesterday, so much had happened that he still hadn't processed it all. He'd bitten Bailey and forged a blood bond, which he then cemented with the most glorious lovemaking he could have imagined. It annoyed him that a morning repeat ended up interrupted by Jaxon, but then again, he couldn't fault the pup, not when he knew his three pack mates were all itching to bind themselves to her and have a taste of their own.

It pleased him to no end to know Wyatt was slowly coming around. Not all matings were lucky enough to have a bond of friendship beforehand. Personally, he thought it made the transition for sharing something so intimate as a woman, and a home, much easier. Knowing she might end up choosing Parker and Jaxon didn't bother him as much as he'd feared. They were men he trusted with his own life, and seeing the protective expressions that had taken up residence on their faces since Bailey had come into their lives, he knew he could trust her well-being with them.

And as for *really* sharing her, while Gavin might have joked with Wyatt about them taking her at the same time, it was only one step from there to wondering about them all coming together in an orgy of bodies. The idea intrigued him. While touching another man held no appeal, he'd found just watching Wyatt kissing Bailey yesterday, as he pleasured her, one of the most erotic experiences of his life. He could only imagine how much more titillating it would be to have more than one man driving her over the edge.

But he was getting ahead of himself. That type of scenario still remained far in the future, so in the meantime, he'd enjoy his one-on-one time with

Bailey. Learning her luscious body . . . tasting her unique flavor . . .

"Would you stop it already?" Wyatt's gruff voice broke into his sensual reverie.

"What?"

"You and that silly grin on your face are going to wrap us around a tree. Keep your mind on the business at hand."

"But it's my business to think of new ways of pleasuring my mate."

"Now you sound like Jaxon."

"Brother, that was so uncalled for. And I have been paying attention, enough to know we're being followed."

"What!" Wyatt craned in his seat and began cursing. "Fuck. Are you sure?"

"Nope, but my wolf seems to think so."

"What are we gonna do?"

A feral smile pulled Gavin's lips taut. "We ambush them first."

* * * *

Bailey couldn't help from lighting up when she saw Gavin and Wyatt strutting into the roadside diner. It especially pleased her that their grim expressions melted into warm smiles of welcome upon seeing her. In short order, she found herself squished in the center of the U-shaped booth, ringed by men. It was enough to render a woman breathless—and make her girly parts moisten.

As the new arrivals ordered, Bailey frowned, noting some contusions on their knuckles and faces, marks that seemed days old, but which she knew neither had sported that morning.

"What happened to you?"

Stretching his arm across the top of her shoulders, Gavin hugged her into him. "Nothing, except I missed you."

"It looks like you were in a fight." She flicked her gaze up to him, but he met her query with a soft smile.

"Nothing Wyatt and I couldn't take care of. Don't worry. You're safe."

"I'm not worried about my safety," she said, her stomach suddenly tight. "I'm worried about you all getting hurt. Was it them? Are they following us?"

She didn't miss the look Gavin and Wyatt shot each other, making it easy to spot the lie when it came.

"Nope. Just some local boys who wanted to play tough. No big deal. Happens all the time."

Dropping her gaze, she tucked her hands in her lap, lest they see them trembling. *Oh my God, those psychos are following us.* Despite Gavin's and Wyatt's assurances, trepidation filled her. She couldn't have said what she ate, although it sat like lead in her stomach.

Exiting the diner, she didn't really pay attention to anything until she found herself ensconced in a different vehicle, with Wyatt and Gavin as her new companions.

Only once they pulled onto the road, Wyatt at the wheel, did Gavin probe her.

"What's wrong, darling?"

"Nothing." Apparently, he didn't believe her lie because he frowned at her.

"I wish you wouldn't lie to me."

The comment annoyed her, and it showed in her tone when she sassed, "Funny, I could say the same thing with your bullshit story of earlier."

Gavin sighed and sat back, rubbing a hand over his face.

"Just tell her the truth," Wyatt said quietly from the front.

"It's all I've ever asked for," she added.

"I don't want to scare you, though." Frustration threaded his reply.

"I'm already terrified, and when you lie, it makes it worse."

"You want the truth? Then fine. We ran into some rogues on the road."

Okay maybe the bald truth wasn't any better. She swallowed hard at the fear that suddenly made her shake and her eyes blur.

"Ah shoot." Brawny arms yanked her until she sat cradled in Gavin's lap. A hand stroked her hair as he murmured to her. "It's going to be all right, darling. We're almost home, and once inside the compound, you won't have to worry."

"So I'll be a prisoner?" she asked through a throat tight with tears.

"Of course not," he retorted. "Although when you do leave, for the first little while at any rate, you'll probably need an escort. But that's pretty standard anyway with all the females, to ensure their safety."

"That still makes me sound like a prisoner."

"Think of it more as a precious princess and her bodyguards."

His analogy made her snort. "Anyone ever tell you that you're full of crap?"

"All the time," Wyatt replied dryly. "But in this case, he's right. Besides, why carry groceries yourself when you can get a man to do it for you?"

Since they didn't seem worried, perhaps she should find her courage and stop acting like such a baby. She straightened in Gavin's lap. "And what will you do when I need to get my hair cut?"

"Get our nails done," Wyatt joked.

"Wax our backs," Gavin added.

As the list of things they'd do continued, getting sillier and sillier, Bailey found her tension easing, but it never completely disappeared, not when she could see them both anxiously glancing in the mirrors at the road behind them, looking for pursuit.

* * * *

Their new campsite looked much like the one of

the night before—lots of woods, no toilets, and filled with men who somehow seemed more vibrant than ever. Watching them from her perch as they set up camp—her feeble attempts to help more like a hindrance—she wondered what made them seem larger than life as they stalked about, filled to the brim with a simmering energy.

It was over a dinner of roasted hot dogs and salad that Gavin casually dropped the bomb. "The full moon's tonight, so we're going to take turns going for a run, if that's okay?"

She almost spat out her mouthful of food. "Say that again?"

Jaxon laughed. "When the moon shines bright, we turn into furry frights."

"Do you want to cuff him, or shall I?" Parker asked Gavin quite seriously.

"Oh, don't hit him," she exclaimed. "It was rather poetic."

A trio of snorts met her words, but Jaxon beamed. "I have another one if you like that. Roses are red, violets are blue, your lips look so juicy, and I'll bet your pus—"

Parker clapped his hand over Jaxon's mouth before he could finish. No matter, Bailey still blushed as she giggled. She laughed even harder at the glares both Wyatt and Gavin threw his way.

"Parker, why don't you take Jaxon for a walk and let his wolf pee on some trees? I mean if he's going to speak like an uncouth animal, then he should act like one."

Jaxon hung his head at their rebuke. She thought him repentant until he winked at her. Bailey bit her lip so as to not give him away.

When he would have left them to do as ordered, Wyatt stopped him and addressed Gavin. "No time like the present for her to see, don't you think?"

Gavin shot her a look and then nodded. "Jaxon, change in front of her, but no funny business, or I'll neuter you myself."

"As you command, oh mighty leader."

A shiver of fear or anticipation, possibly both, went up her spine as Jaxon, with a smirk, began to unbutton his shirt and pulled it off, revealing a smooth, cocoa-colored chest. Lean muscles made his stomach taut and tapered down to lean hips. When she would have looked away as his hands went to his pants, Gavin, who'd come up behind her, tilted her head back.

"You need to watch. Within our community, nudity is not considered taboo, not given our need to let our beasts out to run. It's something you need to get used to."

Unbelievable, I've been commanded by my lover to watch another man undress. Surreal didn't begin to describe it, but once she allowed herself to gaze upon him with cheeks that burned hot, she soon realized she couldn't have dragged her gaze away even if she wanted to. Jaxon kicked off his shoes and shucked off his slacks, standing only in his tight emerald-green briefs.

"Jeez, man, what are you, part leprechaun?" said Wyatt with clear disdain.

Grabbing his crotch, Jaxon leered. "What's wrong? Jealous of my lucky charms?"

Bailey giggled, a laughter cut short as she noticed the bulge in the tight briefs growing. Startled, her eyes rose to meet Jaxon's, who, of course, smiled.

"Enough," Gavin barked. "Can we get on with this?"

"Aye, aye, Captain." Jaxon's tone emerged mockingly. However, the look in his eyes appeared anything but as he skimmed his briefs down. Bailey didn't let her gaze stray from his, despite her curiosity at what he'd uncovered. Then it was all she could do not to scream as he *changed*.

The usual jovial expression on his face turned into a grimace of pain as his body contorted, his shape and skin rippling and reforming into something squatter and thicker. Thick black hair sprouted along every inch of his skin. The whole process took only moments, and when done, a black wolf with intense green eyes stared at her.

Bailey released the breath she held. "That looks like it hurt."

"It does," replied Gavin starkly. "But you get used to it."

For some reason that made her sad. She didn't think she could handle what seemed like excruciating pain on a regular basis. "He looks like the wolf from the woods. The one who saved me."

A bob of the wolf's head acknowledged her statement. Then he lolled his tongue at her and yipped.

"What did he say?" she asked, craning to look at Gavin.

"Something to the effect of you can thank him by rubbing his belly."

Putting actions to words, Jaxon threw himself on his back with his four legs in the air.

Laughter bubbled from her. "Oh my God, he's like a giant puppy."

"Hence his nickname," Parker rumbled.

"Can I touch him?" Before she'd even finished asking, a wet nose nudged her palm. She gasped but didn't withdraw, instead letting her fingers stroke over the soft fur of his pelt. "You're beautiful."

"And I'm jealous," Gavin said wryly. "If I'd known you'd take it so well, I'd have changed first and let you pet me."

"You'll get your turn," she sassed, throwing him a wink. "And more . . ."

Sensing the attention had drifted from him, Jaxon sat on his haunches and let out a short howl.

"Not in camp, you idiot. Get your ass out into the woods if you're going to make noise." Permission granted, Jaxon bounded off into the trees.

"I want you to go with him," Gavin told Parker.

"No problem. I've been itching to go for a run."

Parker seemed more self-conscious than Jaxon at stripping in front of her, his fingers fumbling with the closures for his clothing. Once she saw him nude, she couldn't understand why. The man surely descended from the titans. Broad chested, with a smattering of hair on his upper body, the man was a Goliath all over—or so she assumed. She didn't quite have the nerve to peek below.

His metamorphosis to beast seemed less painful than Jaxon's transition, and damn, did he appear huge. He sported a brown pelt and the same calm eyes she'd grown to know. This time, she went to the wolf and let her fingers stroke the silky fur between his ears. He seemed to like that because he leaned his big head against her and nearly toppled her over. With a chuckle, she kept her balance.

"I think you're even bigger than those wolves in *Twilight*," she complimented, although judging by his chuff and the head-shaking disbelief on Wyatt's face, that wasn't perhaps the right thing to say.

"Off with you now before Jaxon gets in trouble," Gavin ordered.

Parker bounded off into the forest, leaving her alone with Gavin and Wyatt.

"So now what?" she asked perhaps a tad too brightly, much too aware of both men and the fact that she now found herself alone with them. Gavin's slow smile left nothing to the imagination. He caught her up in his arms and kissed her, making his intentions even clearer.

"Shall we?" he asked, inclining his head toward the tent.

"But what about Wyatt?" she whispered.

"He's more than welcome to join us if you'd like."

The shocking suggestion made her flush with heat, and not just in the cheeks. She darted a glance over to see Wyatt staring at her, his head tilted in question.

"I—I—" A part of her wanted to say yes, but she couldn't do it. Not yet. Titillating as it sounded, a part of her still balked at the idea of being intimate with two men at once.

As if reading her chagrin, Wyatt sent her a slow smile. "When you're ready, sunshine, I'll be here. I can wait as long as you need."

Feeling bad, she tucked her face into the curve of Gavin's neck and felt him move away. Ducking into the tent, he'd no sooner tossed her on the air mattress than his body covered hers, his mouth hot and hard against her own.

Arousal immediately flooded her, and she clung to him tightly as she returned his embrace.

The kiss ended up short-lived, as barking suddenly erupted outside the tent.

"Gavin!" Wyatt yelled. "Parker's holding off some rogues."

"Shit!" Rolling off her, Gavin exited the tent, Bailey only seconds behind. She found Jaxon, wearing his man shape, in the clearing, bleeding from a deep gash in his shoulder while Wyatt and Gavin both stripped.

"They caught me unawares," Jaxon explained, holding a hand to his wound. "I was fighting them off when Parker arrived. He told me to get you."

"You did the right thing," Gavin said, removing his underwear and standing in the nude.

"What are you doing?" she asked in a quavering voice as it suddenly came to her that he was leaving.

"What the council's assigned us to do. Eliminate rogues."

"Eliminate . . ." Her eyes widened in horror. "You mean kill them?"

"I don't have time to go into the whys or specifics right now," Gavin replied. "I'll explain it later. For now, go in the tent and into my knapsack. There's a revolver loaded with silver in there. Take it. If anything furry comes out of those woods, shoot it."

"But—"

He planted a hard kiss on her lips. "Please, darling. Just do as I say. I'm leaving Jaxon here to protect you, but we won't be far, so scream if you need us."

Any more words of protest she might have spewed died in her throat as Gavin stepped away and shifted, more quickly than his friends, into a beautiful golden wolf. A black wolf with a familiar cynical gaze came to stand beside him, and they bounded off into the encroaching gloom. Disbelief and fear rooted her to the spot.

"Don't just stand there," Jaxon croaked. "Get the gun."

"Where's the first aid kit?" she asked instead of obeying.

"In the knapsack. Now move."

She dove into the tent and found Gavin's bag. Dragging it out, she plopped it beside Jaxon before rummaging in it. The fast-approaching darkness, though, impeded her search. With a sigh of annoyance, she upended the bag and found the pistol but nothing resembling a first aid kit.

"I can't find it," she wailed in frustration.

"Because we don't have one in camp," he admitted.

Gritting her teeth, she tried not to lose her temper. "Then why did you say there was?"

Instead of an answer, he handed her the gun by the butt, and her eyes widened. "That was a naughty trick, Jaxon. You need medical care more than I need to shoot myself in the foot."

"I'll be fine. A little bit of moonlight, and maybe a kiss, will make it better."

She stuck her tongue out at him and laid the gun on the ground as she bent to find a clean T-shirt that she could at least use to wipe his wound, anything to distract her from what might be going on in the woods.

The moon came out, easing her task as its luminous glow lit up the clearing and bathing her in its cool radiance. An itch made her twitch her nose, then scrunch her face up, as her skin erupted in the most unpleasant sensation, as if bugs crawled across her skin. With a soft cry, she dropped her makeshift cloth and rubbed at her face.

"Bailey?"

A cry left her lips, and she fell to her knees as pain rippled through her, a burning agony that ignited all of her nerve endings at once. She screamed, unable to help herself, and then thrashed as constricting hands tried to hold her. Another scream escaped her then another.

"Noooo!" An alien presence pushed forth in her mind, striving to take over, and for a moment, vivid red eyes flashed before her. And then she felt her whole world twist. Her panting cries of pain transitioned into a . . . howl.

Oh my God. Oh my God. The mantra kept repeating itself in almost incoherent gibberish in her mind. Something touched her still-throbbing sides, and without thinking, she turned her head and snapped. She caught something fleshy in her teeth, and she bit down hard, a warm spurt of fluid coating her tongue. Enjoying the taste, she chomped down harder, but something pried her jaw open, and the meat pulled free. Enraged at having her meal taken away, she attacked, her claws striking the animal before her, gouging its thin skin. The scent of blood, a smell she finally recognized, filled her senses and made her slaver in hunger.

A harsh noise beat at her ears, though, the sound familiar, and . . .

Regaining control of her mind, Bailey recoiled in horror from Jaxon, the severely injured Jaxon, who yelled at her to stop.

What have I done? Or the even better question, what had she become?

Releasing a scream that emerged as a mournful howl, she turned and ran into the woods, ignoring Jaxon's cries for her to return.

She could never go back. *I am a monster.*

Chapter Eleven

Coasting through the woods, following the trail Jaxon left in drops of blood, Wyatt let his fury against rogues build. *Why won't they leave her alone? Why are they still brazenly chasing her?* It baffled him. Rogues weren't known to go after complicated targets. So what was it about Bailey that made them keep coming? What did Roderick want from her?

The time to ponder those questions would have to wait, as he came across the snarls of animals sparring.

Springing into the fray, he took in the scene, from Parker grappling viciously with a mottled-coated foe to the others circling, preparing to launch their own cowardly attack. Assessing the imminent danger to his friend, Wyatt landed on the back of a wolf who thought to attack Parker from behind while Gavin, with a snarl to frighten all but the most foolhardy, dove at the rest to keep them at bay.

A bestial part of himself rejoiced in the yelp of pain of his enemy as his teeth sank into flesh. Bloodlust and the exhilaration of battle suffused him, and he gleefully tore into the attacking wolves, whose paltry number of eight were no match for the three of them. The one he'd attacked went still as he snapped its neck finally with his powerful jaw, and he went on to the next. As the fifth and sixth miscreants fell to the ground, leaking their life's blood into the earth, the last two took off running, probably sensing their imminent defeat. *Run, you little bastards, all you want. You'll never escape us.*

Parker and Gavin took off after them, but Wyatt took an extra moment to check the still bodies to make sure none played possum. His father had taught him at a young age to always make sure he never left any of the enemy alive lest they sneak up when least expected. After determining their glazed-eyed death real and not faked, Wyatt made to follow his pack brothers when a shrill scream rang through the forests, followed by another.

Wyatt stumbled. *Bailey!* What to do, he had a duty to his alpha, to capture the escaping rogues. But to chase them meant abandoning Bailey.

Like fuck.

It took him only a moment to decide before tearing back through the woods toward camp, a howl rolling out of his throat, announcing his intention. Gavin and Parker didn't answer or follow, the renewed sounds of battle rising behind him. Seesawing in his mind, a part of him wondered if he should return to give them aid, but he already knew what Gavin would tell him. *Protect Bailey.* It's what any mate would order. *And what I need to do.*

The shrieking, a chilling sound filled with agony, continued, only to abruptly cut off, replaced by a mournful howl that raised his hackles. *What the fuck? Did some rogues circle around us to attack the camp?*

Bursting through the underbrush, Wyatt charged into the clearing with the tents and skidded to a halt. Switching forms quicker than he ever recalled doing before, he scanned the immediate area, and he inhaled deeply, scenting blood. The owner of the fluid appeared to be Jaxon, sprawled and bleeding from numerous wounds.

"What happened? Where's Bailey?" Wyatt barked. He recognized the signs of a wolf attack, the long scratches on Jaxon's torso, along with dentition marks on his arm. The pup would heal, but only if Wyatt let him live after he found Bailey unharmed. "Which way did they go?"

"No one else," mumbled Jaxon as he pulled himself upright, his face grimacing in pain. "She changed."

"What do you mean changed?" Wyatt sniffed the air and caught a wolf scent, a she-wolf one that seemed vaguely familiar.

"Bailey's a fucking wolf. As soon as the moonlight hit her, she started screaming, and then . . ."

She morphed. And judging by the tenor of her screams, not only was it excruciating but she was also probably terrified because she didn't understand what was happening. Horror made Wyatt speechless. It was one thing to grow up knowing and expecting the transition, another to go through it without knowledge or preparation.

He needed to find her and help her through this unexpected event. "Where is she now?"

"How the fuck should I know? Or did you not notice my injuries?" Jaxon snarled. "I tried to hold her back, talk to her, you know? But she attacked me, and I was so shocked, I didn't fight back. I didn't want to hurt her." Frustration colored his words

"She didn't mean to injure you. She was scared."

"Well duh, man. I know that, but she got me good enough that I couldn't follow. And besides, I thought someone needed to know what happened. What I don't understand is how it happened. I thought she wasn't wolf."

"She wasn't. She must have been a dormant." A sleeping wolf triggered by her proximity to her mates? He'd never heard of it happening before, but then again, he'd never heard of a wolf being born to humans.

"A dormant raised among humans?" Jaxon raised the very question he'd just asked himself.

"I don't have time to figure this out. I need to go after her."

"I'll go with you."

Wyatt shot him a wry look. "Injured as you are? I don't think so. You stay here and wait for the others. Let them know what's happened. Gavin will be able to follow my trail, and I'll signal when I've found her."

For a moment, Wyatt expected the pup to argue,

but he must have hurt more than he let on because he nodded with his lips drawn tight. "Watch yourself, Wyatt. Her wolf's quite the bitch."

Wyatt bared some teeth in a feral grin. "Perfect." Shifting back into his beast, the moon's glow aiding him in what would have taxed him on a regular day, he let his wolf take over, trusting its instincts to track their woman.

The path he followed meandered through the woods, the mad dash of an animal confused and maddened by pain. Wyatt's heart ached as he saw the signs of her agitation. *If only we'd known this was possible, we would have never left her alone.*

Her transformation did answer a few questions, though, such as why the rogues wanted her— females were always prime prey for any Lycan. It also explained why the four of them had found themselves inexplicably drawn to her. *She was never human to start with.*

It did raise an interesting concern about her, though, such as, how did a dormant come to live with humans in the first place? The mother's missing information, he'd bet, was a clue that he'd have to look into, once he found Bailey that was.

It took him an hour of running and hunting before he caught sight of her, her steps slowing as she bounded on four legs through the forest. He yipped to catch her attention, but it didn't have the effect wanted. Instead of stopping and facing him, she renewed her speed, bolting heedlessly. Wyatt followed. It was all he could do.

He just hoped in their mad flight they didn't accidentally run across any more rogues—or something worse.

Wolves might have natural predator tendencies, but some things were bigger on the food chain, like bears, for one, and he definitely never wanted to tangle with any wildcats again. They had some nasty razor-sharp claws.

On and on they ran, Bailey's steps growing more and more sluggish until they stopped altogether as she reached a riverbank with a swift-flowing current. She stopped and whirled, her eyes peering frantically from side to side, the gaze of a trapped animal. Advancing on her slowly, he noted when she realized she'd lost her chance to escape. Her lips peeled back from her gums, and she growled, the hackles on her back rising.

Not wanting to get into a fight with her, and possibly injure her, he slowed his pace and halted a few feet from her. He lay down in front of her, resting his head on his paws, and just looked at her, trying to appear as nonthreatening as possible.

Bit by bit, her aggressive stance receded until, with a whine, she collapsed, burying her muzzle between her paws. Easing forward carefully, he slunk across the ground until he crouched before her. He rubbed his nose against her, and she whimpered, her whole frame shaking. Encouraged, he licked her fur with his raspy tongue, soothing her in the only way he could in this form. He didn't dare change back yet, not when she could decide to bolt at any moment—or snap.

He crawled as carefully as possible to prevent startling her and then pivoted until he lay alongside her. She leaned into him, still shivering, and he breathed a sigh of relief in his mind when she fell asleep.

Slumber eluded him, though, as he watched and waited. He realized he'd never given an audible signal for Gavin to follow, but he couldn't let that worry him. Keeping Bailey calm and safe was all that mattered for the moment. His friend possessed a keen nose. He'd find them.

Lying beside the she-wolf he longed to call his own, now more than ever, he wondered if this drastic change would make her more likely, or less, to bond with them. Previously, when he'd thought her human, he'd enjoyed knowing that if she chose him, the reason would center around a mutual affection between them.

Now that she'd turned Lycan, would emotions still factor into her decision, or would her bestial side make the choice for her?

Did it matter?

I discovered my feelings for her before I ever knew she was pack. Judging by her responses to me, I think she felt the same things I did. Sure, those feelings would probably seem more exaggerated with her beast now making its own demands, but he could content himself with knowing, change or not, she'd have eventually come to him and learned to care for him the same way he had for her.

It must be love if it can have me being so sappy even in my own mind. I sound like Gavin. And he didn't care. As she snuggled deeper against him, her trust in him warmed his heart and reaffirmed his decision to bond with her.

Lycan or human, short acquaintance, and crazy or not, he would become a part of Bailey's life, as her mate and lover.

* * * *

Excruciating pain woke her, a familiar agony that made her think of evil red eyes and the cell she'd been shackled in.

What the hell?

The image of a cadaverous, grinning facsimile of a man faded in her mind, replaced by the blazing light of agony as her body melted back into her human self. Awash with sobs, and shaking like a leaf in a strong wind, it took her a few moments to realize arms held her, rocking her. She clutched the body that offered her comfort, anything to help dispel the nightmare. Unfortunately, her mind would give her no respite and kept replaying over and over her horrible change and then . . . the blood. *Oh God, the blood.*

"Jaxon!" she wailed, the realization of what she'd

done making her sob anew.

"Hush, Bailey. He's going to be fine. He's a tough bugger. But what about you? Are you okay?"

Hysterical laughter threatened to burst forth, and her eyes filled with tears. "N-N-No, I'm n-n-not all right," she stuttered. "Oh my God, Wyatt. It hurt so bad. Still hurts." An ache that went deep into her bones, muscles, and even stranger, her mind, where an alien presence now hovered, whimpering.

"I know the pain, sunshine. The first few times are the worst."

"First?" Panic made her lift her head and regard him with wild eyes. "No. No. No." She shook her head, sending her hair flying in all directions. "I can't do that again. I refuse."

"I don't think you'll have a choice. It would seem you hid a wolf inside you all this time. And now that she's been released, you'll never be without her again."

As if sensing he spoke about her, the foreign presence in her mind perked up and rumbled softly. It didn't reassure her. "But I don't want a wolf!" Bailey cried. "I want to be me, Bailey Donovan, chubby girl with a boring job. Not a werewolf. I can't be a monster."

"Well, you know what they say. You can't always get what you want," he replied wryly. "And you're not a monster."

"Says the man who thinks turning into some murdering animal is okay."

He tightened his arms around her, and his voice came out low with a repressed fury she could almost taste and that made her new wolf growl. "We. Are. Not. Monsters. Do you understand me?" He shook her lightly.

"What happened last night between you and Jaxon was an accident because you panicked. It won't happen again because, next time, you'll be prepared."

"Prepared?" she scoffed. "Nothing will ever prepare me for a pain so intense I want to kill myself."

"It will get easier."

"Says you. And how am I supposed to deal with the dog in my mind?"

"First off, she's not a dog or a monster. She's your wolf, an intrinsic part of you, and calling her names will hurt her feelings."

The wolf in her mind paced and seemed to nod in agreement, soundly chastising Bailey for her rude outburst.

"I'm sorry. But this is all so strange. I-I don't feel like me anymore."

"But you are," he whispered in her ear. "You are a very special woman, Bailey Donovan. Never forget that."

Unsettled by his words, she pushed from him and stood only then noticing her nude state. Slapping hands over body parts, she tried to cover herself, which made Wyatt chuckle. He stood, and her eyes widened as she took in his naked frame. What a lovely eyeful that was. It directed her thoughts to things other than her new Lycan status.

"I think it's rather late for modesty," he said, reaching out to grab her hands and pry them loose.

She resisted at first, but his greater strength peeled her hands away, and he reeled her in until she stood against him—flesh to flesh. Oh, the decadent heat and hungers that roused in her. The presence in her mind seemed to whisper to her, *Bite him. Mark him. Make him ours*. It frightened her.

"Why is this happening to me, Wyatt? Why now? Why me?" she asked, staring at the hollow of his neck, trying hard to control the tears that threatened.

"I don't know, sunshine. Maybe being with us triggered it, or maybe you were always meant to change. I guess we'll ever know why. The important thing is you are not alone. I know that first time was real scary, mostly because you weren't prepared. It will get easier. We'll help, all of us, in any way we can. You're pack now. And pack sticks together."

"I'm so scared," she whispered before burying her face against the smooth skin of his chest, reassured by the steady beat of his heart, although it did nothing to stop her tears from wetting him.

"You're not alone," he murmured, his big hands stroking up and down the skin of her back.

It took his soothing touch for her to realize the pain of her change no longer troubled her. In fact, she felt great. On the heels of those realizations came a shiver as she took notice of her position. Naked, her skin brushed against Wyatt's, and where it touched, it began to burn, not the painful kind, but the type of heat that made her cleft moisten. She waited for the wolf in her mind to ruin the moment with some weird possessive claim, but she remained silent, nothing to distract her from her growing arousal.

As if sensing the change in her, Wyatt's hand tilted her chin up, and he stared at her with dark eyes, his desire clear to see. She could see the question in his gaze, and in that moment, the answer was easy.

"I'm ready," she stated, so low she thought he might not have heard. He stood rock still for a few seconds, and then, her words must have sunk in because his lips swooped to claim hers in a heady kiss that made her reel.

Hunger flooded her, and need, a need to feel him sinking inside of her. A need to reaffirm she lived.

She twined her fingers in his hair, opening her mouth to let his tongue sweep in and drag along hers, making her tingle. A hard and thick thigh inserted itself between her legs and rubbed against her pussy. A gasp escaped her, caught by his mouth, as he dragged his limb across her sensitive cleft, teasing her.

"Wyatt," she keened.

"More?" he teased.

His lips lefts hers, and bending her backward

slightly, he trailed them down to her chest, circling around her globes. She panted, her fingers curling and digging into his muscled shoulders. As if sensing her impatience, he chuckled, and his warm breath feathered across her nipples, making her shiver. He caught one of the tight buds in his mouth, sucking it and then biting down on it gently. She cried out as it sent a jolt right down to her sex.

"Like that, did you?" he murmured and then did it again.

Her hips bucked, and she mewled in need. He didn't let go of her nipple, instead inhaling it deeper into his mouth as his leg left the warm cradle of her thighs. But she didn't mourn its loss for long because his fingers took their place, alternately stroking then plucking at her clit, driving her wild.

When he finally stopped the torture to grasp her buttocks and hoist her, she was more than ready. Her legs wrapped around his waist, but his cock ended up missing her cleft and sitting below her buttocks. She squirmed, and Wyatt chuckled.

"Impatient, sunshine?"

"Wyatt . . ." She drew his name out on a frustrated sigh that had him adjusting their position until the head of his shaft butted against her sex. Tightening her limbs around him, she drew him into her body and sighed as he stretched her passage.

A low groan rumbled from him, and his fingers tightened on her ass once he ended up fully sheathed. "Oh, damn, sunshine. You feel so fucking good."

His words made her plaster her mouth against his, wanting the taste of him to fill all her senses. Still standing, a position he handled with ease, even given her curves, he began to thrust in and out of her. She gasped. How incredible it felt. He tortured her by pulling his shaft out halfway, only to then slam himself home, jolting her and making her pussy tighten convulsively around him.

In and out he pumped, driving her desire up and up until she keened breathlessly, waiting for that moment she'd fall off the edge. At the periphery of her pleasure, she could feel the alien presence, her wolf. It threw her for a moment, but the pleasure soon made her ignore it, and then forget it, as her climax hit and sent all thought racing out of her head.

With a scream of pleasure, she came apart in his arms, her body trembling as her sex milked him. As she hovered in the moment, vulnerable and open, the presence within her pushed forth and made her sink her teeth into his shoulder, biting hard enough to break skin. Almost immediately, Wyatt reciprocated, biting down on her shoulder.

Blood hit her tongue, and she swallowed without thinking before wrenching herself away with a cry.

It didn't matter at that point. She heard an almost audible snap as some kind of esoteric circle shut and bound her to Wyatt, just like it had with Gavin. When Wyatt released her sated body, letting her feet hit the ground, she looked up to see him beaming uncharacteristically.

He kissed the tip of her nose and whispered, "Thank you, sunshine, for choosing me. I promise to cherish you forever."

Suddenly fighting tears, she threw herself at him for a bone-crushing hug.

Okay, whether I intended to or not, I think I just married my second husband. The idea didn't freak her out as much as it should have.

Chapter Twelve

Gavin breathed a sigh of relief when he came across Bailey and Wyatt, thankfully unharmed, the cries he'd heard those of the mating kind. He slapped Wyatt on the back as he curled an arm around Bailey's waist.

"Congrats."

A blush pinked her cheeks, and Gavin laughed as he kissed her to show her that he wasn't bothered by her newest mate. "Relax, darling. I'm not going to go into a jealous fit and challenge Wyatt or anything."

"That's good," she replied softly. Then her expression turned morose. "How's Jaxon? Wyatt said he'd be okay. Is he very angry?"

"A better question is, should he be punished for letting you run off in the first place?" Gavin growled, still not over his anger when he'd found out what happened after he dispatched the rogues and returned to camp.

"It's not his fault," she said, jumping to his defense. "Nobody knew I was going to-to . . ." Her voice trailed off, and she bit her lip.

"It's not an embarrassing disease, sunshine," Wyatt supplied in the silence. "Or do you think there's something wrong with us?"

"No, of course not. It's just"—she paused and looked at each of them—"my whole world has collapsed around me. I don't know what to believe anymore or what's going to happen. I'm scared of changing again, terrified, actually, of the pain. Wyatt says I can learn how to control myself, but what if I hurt someone again when I do morph? It's great Jaxon healed, but what if he'd been human?"

"This is why we need to get home, the sooner, the better. There are people there who are better suited for helping you to understand the things happening within your mind and body as you adjust to sharing yourself with your Lycan side. It's also a safe environment for you to shift and learn some control."

"If you say so."

Gavin could see the doubt still in her eyes, but he didn't have time to quell it. They needed to get moving before more rogues arrived. He and Parker might have dispatched the stragglers the previous night, but the last one to die had, for a moment, turned into a puppet for Roderick who'd taunted him with a, "Run, run as fast as you can. I'll still catch you because I'm the bogeyman."

The mutated childhood rhyme still made him want to shiver. He wouldn't feel safe until Bailey resided safe and secure behind the fortification of the pack's compound.

He and Wyatt took turns carrying her back to

camp despite her protests. Seeing as how she found herself barefoot and naked, he didn't want her getting scratched up and bruised even if he knew she would heal. And women claimed chivalry was dead.

When they reached camp, her body tensed in his arms. Knowing words would mean nothing, Gavin tilted his head to Jaxon, who held out his arms so he could hand her over.

A gasp escaped her, and Gavin watched as her eyes dropped, still fearful of Jaxon's reaction—and condemnation. But if he knew Jaxon, he would turn her misery around in no time.

"Sweet cheeks! You're back, you sexy vixen you," Jaxon exclaimed.

"I'm so sorry," she managed to choke out.

"For what? Getting frisky? No worries. I wish I'd known you liked it rough. I would have brought my handcuffs. Besides, it would take more than a beautiful she-wolf nibbling on my man parts to bring me down," he joked with a waggle of his brows.

"But I tried to eat you," she whispered, not ready to forgive herself.

"I wish," Jaxon replied with a heartfelt sigh.

Her head shot up, and Gavin laughed at the expression on her face. "I told you he was fine. Now, can we all get moving? I know it's not quite dawn, but I think it best if we got on the road and back to the compound ASAP."

At her urging, Jaxon let Bailey down, and she

looked around, biting her lip. Her cheeks shone a ruddy red.

"Um, I'm all for leaving, but I don't suppose I could have some clothes to wear first. I'd really hate to stick to your leather seats."

The laughter eased the last of their tension, and Gavin began to hope that all would turn out all right with his mate. Her change might have taken them all by surprise, and she might have some reservations about her newfound status, but he'd seen the strong spirit she harbored. With time, and affection, she'd eventually accept her inner wolf. She had two mates who would make sure of it.

* * * *

The closer they got to their final destination, the more Bailey's stomach tightened into a ball. Despite what she'd learned about the compound, and the reassurances of her lovers, whom she rode with, she found herself terrified. *Oh God, what am I getting myself into?*

In spite of her fears, she couldn't deny she needed to go there, needed to find out what had happened to her and her body. And, if she were really truthful with herself, she didn't want to leave Gavin and Wyatt. Actually, she didn't want to leave any of them, and she didn't have just her new inner wolf to blame for that.

She enjoyed being around them. They made her

feel alive in a way she'd never felt, even when her parents lived. The passion both Gavin and Wyatt showed her blew her away. The kind of pleasure she discovered with them was usually reserved for romance books, not overweight call-center operators, which brought to mind another thing. With them, she never felt fat.

Tom, her scuzzy ex, had enjoyed making snide remarks about her size, and while it hurt, she'd put up with it because she'd harbored those same self-doubts. However, Gavin and Wyatt made her feel beautiful. They desired her and showed her proof of their appreciation for her curves with every touch and heated look. Even more amazing, they weren't alone or an aberration. Jaxon and Parker held the same admiration and weren't afraid to show it. Acceptance for her as she was made dealing with other things, like, say, her new canine side, a little easier to bear. Of course, she might think differently the next time she went through the pain of the change or tried to take a chunk out of someone else.

Her relief when she'd discovered Jaxon was none the worse for wear after her inexcusable mauling eased her fear somewhat, but the fading scars on his body reminded her that her new life was fraught with dangers, and not all of them external. But she could learn. *No, I will learn.*

It was the only way to keep the wonderful and fascinating men in her life. *Men who are about to see me puke,* she thought, slapping a hand on her mouth as her stomach lurched, her unease tripling as the SUV went through some gates into what had to be the compound.

"We're home," Gavin announced, turning to smile at her.

She could only nod her head sickly, trying not to embarrass herself. *There's nothing to fear. There's nothing to fear.* She kept chanting that mantra as they helped her out of the truck. Wyatt slid an arm around her waist while Gavin talked in a low tone to Parker and Jaxon, who had parked alongside them. Her rah-rah chant died when a dark-haired beast of a man, flanked by two almost equally imposing men, came striding toward them sporting a formidable glower.

"Did you have any more trouble on the way?" the stranger barked.

Bailey flinched and tried to move back. Wyatt peeked down at her and frowned. "There's nothing to fear, sunshine. That's just Nathan, our pack alpha and council leader."

"You forgot blunt idiot," said a woman's voice dryly. Bailey lifted her head to see a trim blonde step out from behind Nathan and the pair of men at his sides. She slapped the guy Wyatt called alpha then came toward Bailey with her hand held out. "Ignore him. His manners seem to disappear in matters where Roderick is concerned. I'm Dana, by the way."

Bailey held out her own hand, and the woman clasped it with a smile that softened her brusque tone. "I'm Bailey."

"Hi there, Bailey. Welcome to the pack. From what I hear, you've had a rough time of it. Why don't you come with me, and I'll get you settled in while these lugs hash things out."

As Dana pulled her away from Gavin and Wyatt, Bailey threw an uncertain look over her shoulder.

Gavin sent her a smile meant to look reassuring. It didn't help the knot of fear in her stomach. "It's okay, darling. Dana doesn't bite, and we'll be along in a bit."

A snort sounded from the handsome blond who'd arrived with Nathan. "Doesn't bite! Ha. That's what you think." At Bailey's wide-eyed look, he grinned. "But don't worry, she saves that particular pleasure for her mates."

"Idiot," Dana muttered, her affection clear despite the rude name. "That's Kody, by the way, one of my mates, along with the ogre, and John, our handsome resident doctor."

Nathan made a face at her remark, but this time it didn't frighten Bailey, for she saw the humor and love in his eyes for Dana.

"You have three mates?"

"Yup. I hear you've got two, with two more waiting in the wings, hoping real hard you'll pick them."

A blush stained Bailey's cheeks. "Um, yeah. Gavin and Wyatt are both my mates, apparently, but Jaxon and Parker have kind of hinted they'd like to be as well."

Dana whirled and pierced her with a searching gaze. "You got a choice, though, right? They didn't force you?"

For a moment, Bailey almost blurted out what Gavin had done to get her to go with them. However, seeing the hard-eyed stare of this no-nonsense woman, Bailey hedged the truth. "I am happy to be their woman, even if it is a really messed-up practice."

A smile curved Dana's lips. "Tell me about it. I ran away from the pack when I was young to avoid having to mate with a bunch of horndogs, but as fate would have it, I came back and ended up caving to pack law by joining with three."

"Do you regret it?" Bailey almost bit her tongue as the presumptuous question popped out.

Dana didn't seem to mind, and her smile widened. "Never. I discovered there are a lot worse things in life than having three men willing to love me and lay down their lives for me. And the sex is wicked," she added with a wink.

Stunned at her comment, Bailey couldn't help the giggle that turned into full-blown laughter as Dana joined her.

In that moment, she discovered not only a friend—or so she hoped—she also found relief. Perhaps things would turn out fine after all.

After that icebreaking moment, Bailey started to pay attention to their surroundings as Dana led her on foot through a well-organized village. Dozens of houses, some covered in vinyl siding while others appeared shingled, dotted the area. Gravel paths, wide enough for two vehicles, made up streets. Dana waved at the slim-figured women and rambunctious children out and about walking, playing, or gardening. Most of them smiled, and all but a few gazed upon Bailey with interest.

Dana didn't stop to chat, which relieved Bailey, as she didn't think she could handle meeting a boatload of people and trying to remember names. It did encourage her, though, to see what looked like regular life going on despite their *unique* condition.

The compound also appeared larger than expected, and Bailey mentioned that to Dana.

"It's grown a lot in the last few years. It's already doubled in size since I came here over three years ago, as we've started to bring in the smaller packs without proper gated communities to merge with the larger established ones. Too many Lycans were going missing, at the hands of Roderick, we have no doubt. Now we're accelerating the merging process because initially, Roderick only went after the weak, one at a time, when they left the security of their packs, but in the last few years, he's begun attacking the smaller enclaves."

"Who's this Roderick you keep mentioning?" The name seemed vaguely familiar, but Bailey couldn't place it.

Dana sent her a puzzled look. "Roderick is

Nathan's father. Or he was. Nathan challenged him for rule of the pack after Roderick went insane and began killing humans. The council at the time claimed to have sentenced him to death, but in truth, they sent him as a gift to the vampire queen."

A short laugh escaped her. "Vampires? You're pulling my leg."

A solemn look dropped over Dana's face. "I wish. We didn't know they existed either until a run-in with Roderick a few years back. After that unpleasant fiasco, Nathan turned pack law against the council for their conspiracy and crimes. They were executed, and Nathan became the new head of council."

Bailey swallowed hard. "You guys don't mess around."

"We can't. Not with the possibility humans would eradicate us if they knew of our existence. I take it the boys didn't tell you any of this?"

Bailey shook her head. "Nope. Why would they?"

"They were supposed to keep an eye out for Roderick while hunting the rogues in your area."

"They found some rogues, all right, but I don't recall them saying anything about this Roderick guy. So what's he after?" For a fleeting moment, it occurred to Bailey to wonder if this Roderick was behind those rogue wolves who kept attacking her. A vision of red eyes flashed in her mind, gone again just as quickly, and taking with it her musings on

Roderick.

Dana's shoulders lifted in a shrug. "Who knows why he does anything? He was a sick bastard when he was sentenced for his crimes against the pack and humanity, and he's an even more sadistic one now that he's a vampire. But you don't need to worry about him anymore. Now that you're with the pack, you're safe."

A shiver went down Bailey's spine, and a superstitious urge to knock on wood assailed her. She knew with a bone-deep certainty that somewhere, Murphy, and his damned law, giggled madly, waiting for his chance. The more she heard claims the compound was safe, the more Bailey started to doubt it. However, she kept her fears to herself. No one needed to know what a paranoid scaredy-cat—um, wolf—she was.

Halting in front of a house finished with pale yellow siding and a white front door, Dana said, "Welcome to your new home."

Staring up at the cute bungalow, Bailey couldn't help but fall in love with it. Of course, it would need a few feminine touches, like white shutters to frame the pair of windows and some flower beds to break the plainness of the front lawn, but all in all, it was picture-book perfect.

So of course, she burst into tears.

Sobbing noisily, she let Dana lead her inside and seat her on a massive leather couch.

"Oh crap. What's wrong? What did I do?" Dana

seemed at a loss as she patted Bailey on the back.

"I-I . . ." Bailey couldn't express what exactly had set her off. The house was adorable. The men ardent. The community welcoming. *So why am I crying like an idiot?* For a moment the answer eluded her, then hit—acceptance, and a sense of coming home.

Since her parents' death, she'd floated along, alone, and despairing of ever feeling whole again. Wanted. In just a few days, she'd gone from nothing and a future of bleakness to a life filled with passion, adventure, and more. Surely it wouldn't last.

"I know it's a lot to take in," Dana said as if reading her mind. "When I came back after being away so long, I kept thinking I'd wake up and everything I'd come to love would disappear and I'd be back on the run, alone and scared."

The words mirrored her thoughts. "What if it doesn't work?" Bailey whispered through a throat tight with tears. "It's all happened so fast. What if they decide they don't want me? Where will I go? What will I do?"

"First off," said Gavin, startling her. She looked up to see him standing in the doorway, having approached them without warning. "I will always want you. Second, this is your home now. Even if you decide you hate me and Wyatt tomorrow, and throw us out on our ears, you never have to leave. Ever." He stressed the last word.

"And three," Wyatt added, joining Gavin in the doorframe. "Haven't you figured it out yet that we love you?"

"You do?" Bailey knew her mouth hung wide open, but she couldn't help it. Their announcement shocked her. "But you barely know me."

"Oh, they know more than you think," Dana stated before standing up. She moved to the door but before leaving paused to say, "You've got to trust somebody sometime. And I can tell you right now, these two men, once they give their word, they don't break it. Don't make the same mistakes I did. Give them a chance. I'll see you tomorrow."

Dana left, and Gavin came into the room and sat beside her. Wyatt followed, taking up position on her other side.

Brushing a strand of hair from her forehead, Gavin leaned into her, rubbing his nose against hers. "Oh, darling, I wish you'd believe me when I say I love you. Can't you see how wonderful you are? How brave?"

"He's right, you know," Wyatt murmured from behind her ear. "Hell, do you think I would have fallen as quickly as I did for you if there wasn't something special about you?"

"Is it me or the whole wolf thing, though?"

"Oh, most definitely you," Gavin whispered against her lips. "I wanted you even when I thought you were the cutest human I'd ever seen."

"I fought wanting you with every ounce of my being, but in the end, how could I resist you?" Wyatt added.

"Even if I'm not skinny like the others?" It hadn't escaped her notice that the women she'd seen during her trek through the compound didn't seem to own any spare fat, unlike her.

"I like your curves. A lot." Gavin's words fluttered across her lips before he took them.

Wyatt pressed in on her other side, his warm breath in the shell of her ear sending delightful shivers through her frame. "Since she doesn't seem to believe us, brother, I think we need to show her."

She didn't have time to question what he meant because the sensual onslaught began. While Gavin claimed her mouth, Wyatt teased her ear and neck. Caught between them, she could only feel . . . and enjoy.

What a decadent delight to have the two of them so ardently embracing her. It didn't even occur to her to protest this surely taboo exploration of her body by both of them at once. On the contrary, when their hands went to her clothing, she aided them in denuding her body, laying herself bare to their electric touch.

And touch her they did. They left no part of her body unexplored. Two sets of hands roamed her skin, raising goose bumps in their path, lighting her nerve endings with fire until she panted. When their mouths latched onto her breasts, one for each, tugging and pulling, she cried out. She couldn't resist opening her eyes and looking down at them, their heads pressed to her breast, one so fair, the other dark. The decadence of it made her breath catch. Gone were the doubts about the rightness or wrongness of having them both at once. Who cared when it felt so good?

She placed her hands on their heads, the contrast of their hair beneath her fingertips fascinating, but not as fascinating as the sudden path their hands took down her body to her thighs. Legs pried apart, she moaned as their fingers circled around her cleft, teasing her lips and skirting her clit. When they each thrust a finger into her, she bucked, a frantic cry escaping her.

In and out they thrust their digits, their counterclockwise motions inside her making her squirm and pant.

"Please. Oh God." She could only incoherently plead at their exquisite torture.

"Who gets to taste first?" Gavin asked.

"I'm oldest," Wyatt said hoarsely. "Isn't it age before beauty?"

Bailey wondered at their words, especially when their fingers left her body. She couldn't help her mewl of displeasure.

"Shh, darling. We're not done with you yet."

She opened her eyes to find Gavin seating himself on the couch, nude, his cock jutting from his thighs. He stroked it for her, and she licked her lips in anticipation.

Rough hands grasped her waist, and her gaze flew forward to find an equally naked and aroused

Wyatt. His eyes smoldered as he lifted her to hold her over Gavin's lap. Gavin's hands grabbed at her thighs, spreading her, exposing her, which in turn made her tremble and her juices flow.

Slowly, ever so slowly, Wyatt lowered her onto Gavin's cock, letting the fat head part her lips and stretch her. They had all the control, and what a turn-on it was. Inch by inch, Wyatt pushed her down on the hard dick until she sat, Gavin's cock fully sheathed and her buttocks resting on his thighs. Placing her feet on either side of his legs, keeping her spread, Gavin then cupped her breasts, his thumbs rubbing over her erect tips. A part of her wanted to close her eyes and throw her head back, basking in the pleasure as he gently rolled his hips under her, swirling his cock ever so deliciously while he pinched her hard nubs. But she couldn't tear her gaze from Wyatt and the way he stroked his cock in front of her, the tip swollen and glistening, begging for a mouth to suck. Her mouth.

He dropped to his knees before her and came almost eye level with her pussy, her pussy that was getting fucked by his friend's cock. It was the most shocking yet intimate moment of her life. And then Wyatt did something so unexpected.

He licked her. Oh God, the sensation. Oral sex rocked on its own. Getting plowed by either of her lovers made her see stars, but combine the two? She couldn't help the keening cry as her body bucked. Caught between the two of them, impaled on a cock, their hands holding her steady, she couldn't escape the lash of his tongue as he flicked it across her clit. She came, hard and furious, her channel milking Gavin's cock as he gasped under her. He undulated faster into her, and Wyatt kept up his oral attention, sucking at her nub, plying her with tongue until she rolled from her first orgasm into her second. And that one just kept going and going until she thought she'd go hoarse and black out from the pleasure of it.

Gavin grunted as he gave a final thrust up into her, the hot splash of his seed marking his culmination, and she thought they were done.

Wrong.

She found herself pulled off Gavin's cock and sitting on the couch, Gavin holding her limp legs wide so that Wyatt could kneel between them. Then it was his turn to fuck her. She should have been spent from her first two orgasms, sore or even sleeping. Instead, she wanted more. Her mouth was caught by Gavin, who plucked at her sensitive nipples as Wyatt's flesh slapped against hers, his thick cock sliding smoothly in and out of her passage, which rippled with aftershocks around him. Diving deep, he butted up against her G-spot, striking it over and over, coiling her pleasure. He wasn't long in coming, his bellow of success coming on the heels of a third orgasm that made her body tighten and arch, her scream so intense it came out as a soundless croak.

Withdrawing, Wyatt climbed onto the couch to snuggle her on one side while Gavin took the other. Boneless, possibly dead, but completely blown away, she let herself slumber against them, their naked, sweaty bodies a surely intriguing pretzel.

Or so she assumed, given Jaxon's comment of, "Hot damn, I think we need a bigger couch."

For once, she was too tired to even blush.

Chapter Thirteen

Lessons on helping Bailey accept her wolf began the next morning, with the decision made that Parker and Dana would act the part of teachers instead of using strangers.

The arrangement suited Parker just fine, as it would allow him to spend time with Bailey. However, he'd imagined it as a pleasant interval spent talking, and maybe flirting. He'd not counted on her fear of the whole shifting process making her ornery.

It took a lot to hold back a sigh of impatience at her now millionth time repeated, "But it hurts."

"I know, baby, but that's only because you're new to the whole shifting experience. Over time, you'll get used to it."

Seated in the shade of a tree, away from the hustle and bustle that comprised daily life in the compound, Bailey sighed and looked down at her lap, where her fingers restlessly weaved together. "So you all keep saying. Might I say that as a pep talk it sucks? Why can't I just stay in this body? I could hide in the basement on full moons and stay away from cars so I don't chase them."

Her rueful smile made him chuckle. "It doesn't

work that way, baby. Once your wolf becomes an active part of your psyche, you need to let it out for the occasional run. If you don't, it will take over when you let your attention lapse, like when you sleep. You don't want to get in a fight for dominance with your wolf. Trust me, it's not a good thing."

He'd seen that happen once before with his great-grandma, who went a little crazy after all her mates died, leaving her alone. She'd refused to change into her beast, saying running wild through the woods reminded her too much of what she'd lost. One day, while she napped, her wolf took over. Even after they caught her, and she switched back to her human shape, she was never the same again. It still made Parker sad to think of her, especially her last days, until her death a few years ago, which she spent vacant-eyed and locked up for her own safety. No, he knew firsthand caging one's wolf in a prison of your own flesh was never the right solution. Now, he just needed to make Bailey understand.

"Gee, this whole Lycan thing is getting more and more attractive all the time," she drawled sarcastically before crossing her arms and pouting. She looked so adorably petulant that Parker couldn't help laughing.

"Oh, baby, I thought Wyatt was a stubborn cuss, but you totally take the cake."

Her reply? A delectable pink tongue stuck out at him. Parker shifted his frame, yet again, to hide his erection, an ever-present problem around the fascinating Bailey. An idea hit him. "You know what? Let's stop talking about the whole shifting thing—"

"Sounds good to me."

"And go straight to some of your new abilities in this form."

That got her attention. "What do you mean by abilities?"

He shook his head and laughed. "Nope, I'm done explaining. This time, you're going to experience."

Her eyes widened, and she shook her head. "I don't know if that's such a good idea."

Sensing her sudden trepidation, he stood and crossed the short distance between them, plopping himself cross-legged on the verdant grass. "This isn't going to hurt one bit," he said, tugging her onto his lap. "But you need to be calm."

"And how is sitting me on your lap supposed to help?" she asked, craning back to look at him, a teasing curve to her lips.

"It doesn't, but it sure beats sitting alone." It warmed him to no end to see the smile that bloomed on her face at his words. Then a shadow of uncertainty.

"What about Gavin and Wyatt? Won't this bother them?"

"It's okay, baby. Remember, this is how it works in the pack. You can choose up to two more males, or not. It's up to you, but I'll be damned if I sit back and do nothing to woo you into selecting me as one of your mates."

"Woo me?" She laughed. "God, that sounds like something out of the Dark Ages."

"Now you've wounded me," he said with a rumbling chuckle. "But enough distracting me with your feminine wiles. I was going to help you discover your new abilities."

She sobered, and he could feel tension tighten her frame, but at least it wasn't him or his size causing her disturbance. Even among Lycans, Parker was considered a big fellow. While some women found his bulk appealing, a greater number—especially humans—tended toward the camp of intimidated. He didn't want Bailey to ever cower out of fear before him. He would never harm a hair on her head and, despite his girth, would always treat her with the gentlest of hands. Or he would once she chose him as a mate.

"Close your eyes," he whispered against her hair, which tickled him like the softest of silk. When she fidgeted—something his cock enjoyed way too much—he grasped her hands and placed them on his thighs. It made him smile to feel the shiver that went through her body accompanied by the faint scent of her arousal. She was not indifferent to him.

"Now, I want you to listen. Listen carefully, and tell me what you hear."

"I hear you telling me to act all Zen-like," she

sassed.

"Baby, I swear I am going to gag you if you don't obey," he said in a mock growl and then immediately fought a vivid image of her mouth eagerly bobbing on his cock.

As if in cahoots with his lusty thinking, she giggled and bounced a bit in his lap, which made him bite back a groan. Did she even know how she affected him? As she snuggled deeper into him with a sigh, he realized she probably did, the vixen.

"Okay, I'll be serious. I hear insects."

"Too easy, keep listening. Expand your senses. Let yourself really hear."

She stopped wisecracking, and her breathing evened. Her words came slowly. "Birds, somewhere to the left. I hear water, something like a stream." Her body leaned forward, and he braced her lest she land on her face in her trance. "Voices. A mother telling Peter to stop bothering his sister."

Parker smiled. Whether she believed it or not, Bailey had tapped into her enhanced hearing. "Go on."

"I hear . . ." She hesitated. "I don't know what I hear, but it's like a thumping sound." Opening her eyes, she craned to look at him. "What is it?"

"Put your ear against my chest."

She scrunched her nose up but did as he said. At first incomprehension clouded her features, then dawning enlightenment. "I heard your heart! But that's impossible." She sat up straight and almost bashed him in the chin.

He narrowly avoided the collision. "No, it's part of your new abilities. Guess what else you can do?"

"Leap a building in a single bound?"

"No, smarty-pants. Read that sign over there."

"What sign?" she asked, turning to follow his pointed finger to a tiny blob of white by the gravel path that ringed the inner part of the village. She laughed. "Are you insane? It's like a postage stamp from here."

"Really? Look again."

A loud sigh escaped her, but she didn't say another word as she gazed at the posted sign. "No parking. Holy shit." She hopped up from his lap and spun to face him, excitement lighting her face. "Okay, now this is getting cool. What else can I do?"

"Sniff."

"I'd rather use a hankie," she joked, but she closed her eyes and took a deep inhalation through her nose and then started coughing. "Oh my God, too much."

Hopping up, Parker stroked her back as she got over her fit. "Oops, I guess I should have chosen a spot a little less ripe," he said with chagrin. Used to sifting smells, he'd not taken in to account how it would affect her for the first time when she truly tried to scent the air around her. The pungent aroma of skunk added a crowning touch.

"It's okay. At least this whole smelling thing explains why I seem to recognize you all even before

I see you."

"You can differentiate our scents?" he asked with surprise.

A flush crept over her cheeks. "Yeah. Weird, huh?"

"Nope," he said, pulling her in for a brief hug. "It just means you're starting to use some of your Lycan abilities even without thinking about it."

"Okay, so that's three of my five senses. Do the other two get a boost too?" she asked.

"Spirit is not a thing you can tangibly touch or see, but we do have the mating bond, which is esoteric in nature."

"I felt it, actually," she said, ducking her head as if shy.

"You can talk about it. It won't rouse my jealousy. This is the pack way, remember? A law we all abide by."

"Yeah, I know, but give a girl brownie points for not trying to shove it in your face," she said, looking up with a grin. "Like I said, when we did that whole biting thing, it's like a circle completed, or snapped shut. And since that time, I kind of feel Gavin and Wyatt in me. Not their thoughts or what they are doing or anything, but I seem to know, more or less, where they are. I can feel some of their emotions too, like when Wyatt is annoyed at Jaxon."

"Everyone can feel that," Parker joked.

"Okay, so that now covers four of my senses. What about the fifth, touch? I can't say as I've noticed a difference there."

A smile curved his lips. "Think of it more as body instead of touch. This is the one facet the boys enjoy and boast of most. Increased strength, speed, and dexterity compared to humans. And, of course, our rapid ability to heal."

"Wait a second. I started healing before you even saved me from those guys in the woods. Doesn't that blow one of the theories that my mating with Gavin triggered my wolf?"

"Ah, but were you healing like that before you met Gavin in the bar?"

"No."

"So, perhaps it was the scent, or the psychic aspect of meeting your mate, that launched it. We'll probably never know for sure, and it doesn't really matter anymore at this point. Now, do you want to dissect the why and how you became a wolf, or do you want to see if you can beat me in a footrace?"

She eyed him up and down. "Your legs are, like, twice the length of mine. There's no way I can beat you."

"Speed isn't just about taking the biggest or fastest steps. A race also relies on the runner's nimbleness, and that is my weak spot. But if it makes you feel better, I will give you a ten-second start. So on your mark, get set, go!"

A squeal escaped her, and with her eyes dancing excitedly, she took off sprinting. Parker watched her form recede into the woods as he counted before taking off after her. Hot damn was she quick. New to her abilities or not, she managed to tap into them with an effortless ease that pleased him. She wouldn't need many lessons in that regard, although when it came to embracing her actual wolf, he got the feeling they still had a ways to go.

Realizing the little vixen had pulled ahead, Parker poured on some more speed that turned into a headlong bull rush when he heard her scream.

Shambling into a clearing near the edge of the compound boundary, he came across Bailey, safe, in the arms of Jaxon, who grinned.

"Look, Parker. I caught me a hottie!"

Bailey's cheeks bloomed, and Parker chuckled, even though a vague sense of disappointment suffused him that he'd not gotten to catch her. He'd planned to kiss her silly when he did.

There was always the next lesson, though.

* * * *

Gavin paced Nathan's office, disturbed by the report he read. He slapped it down on the desk with a curse.

"How the fuck could we not know this was possible?"

"Care to explain?" Wyatt asked, seated in a casual pose. Only Gavin's long acquaintance with him let him know his friend was anything but.

John, Nathan's second-in-command and pack

doctor, launched into a summary. "We've been digging into Bailey's roots. We first traced her father's line since it was easy, given we had his last name and date of birth. Nothing jumped out at us. He's a born and bred American, from a long line of humans. Where it got tricky was when it came to tracing the mother."

Over the last few days, as Bailey settled into pack living, Gavin and Wyatt had unobtrusively gleaned information from her on her family. What little she knew, that was. Having wanted to keep her good humor intact, and her fear at bay, they'd decided against outright questioning. It had taken longer, but Gavin considered it well worth it given the smiles she greeted them with every day—and the passion she shared with them at night.

Back to the situation at hand, though, they'd managed to pry the knowledge that Bailey's mother, Mary Jean, born Mary Jean Smith, claimed no family living. Worse, without her birth certificate or license, they had to literally dig from scratch to find anything out.

John continued with his summary. "Mary Jean wasn't born in a hospital. Actually, until she was about twenty, Mary Jean didn't seem to exist at all."

"So she changed her name?"

"Nope. She kept it the same, which is the only reason why we discovered there used to be a Mary Jean Smith with the same date of birth who used to live with a small Maine pack."

taking off after her. Hot damn was she quick. New to her abilities or not, she managed to tap into them with an effortless ease that pleased him. She wouldn't need many lessons in that regard, although when it came to embracing her actual wolf, he got the feeling they still had a ways to go.

Realizing the little vixen had pulled ahead, Parker poured on some more speed that turned into a headlong bull rush when he heard her scream.

Shambling into a clearing near the edge of the compound boundary, he came across Bailey, safe, in the arms of Jaxon, who grinned.

"Look, Parker. I caught me a hottie!"

Bailey's cheeks bloomed, and Parker chuckled, even though a vague sense of disappointment suffused him that he'd not gotten to catch her. He'd planned to kiss her silly when he did.

There was always the next lesson, though.

* * * *

Gavin paced Nathan's office, disturbed by the report he read. He slapped it down on the desk with a curse.

"How the fuck could we not know this was possible?"

"Care to explain?" Wyatt asked, seated in a casual pose. Only Gavin's long acquaintance with him let him know his friend was anything but.

John, Nathan's second-in-command and pack

doctor, launched into a summary. "We've been digging into Bailey's roots. We first traced her father's line since it was easy, given we had his last name and date of birth. Nothing jumped out at us. He's a born and bred American, from a long line of humans. Where it got tricky was when it came to tracing the mother."

Over the last few days, as Bailey settled into pack living, Gavin and Wyatt had unobtrusively gleaned information from her on her family. What little she knew, that was. Having wanted to keep her good humor intact, and her fear at bay, they'd decided against outright questioning. It had taken longer, but Gavin considered it well worth it given the smiles she greeted them with every day—and the passion she shared with them at night.

Back to the situation at hand, though, they'd managed to pry the knowledge that Bailey's mother, Mary Jean, born Mary Jean Smith, claimed no family living. Worse, without her birth certificate or license, they had to literally dig from scratch to find anything out.

John continued with his summary. "Mary Jean wasn't born in a hospital. Actually, until she was about twenty, Mary Jean didn't seem to exist at all."

"So she changed her name?"

"Nope. She kept it the same, which is the only reason why we discovered there used to be a Mary Jean Smith with the same date of birth who used to live with a small Maine pack."

"What?" Wyatt's shock mirrored his own when he'd read that tidbit. "Why would they let a she-wolf leave?"

Nathan's fingers drummed on his desktop. "They didn't, or did it not occur to you that a Lycan female cannot produce a child with a human?"

"So she was a dormant," Gavin concluded. "But since when do dormants birth wolves?"

"I think the better question," John said, "is how many more latent wolves are roaming around out there?"

For a moment stunned silence reigned before their voices all rang out in a cacophony of sound where no one was heard.

"Silence." Nathan's command cut through their chatter. "I think it's becoming clear that dormants might not be the nonwolves we once thought. Dana herself was believed to be one until she shifted abruptly in her late teens. Bailey is another example."

"It should be noted that, in both cases, the women had met their mates. For Dana, she required an intimate act to trigger it, followed by a full moon, while Bailey just needed for her wolf to sense her mate or, in this case, mates. Could we have been wrong all this time? Could it be that some latents only develop in the presence of their mates?"

The implication . . . damn. Gavin didn't even want to think what it meant. "So we could have any number of people running around with the Lycan gene. Walking time bombs that could go off if they have sex with the right person. How reassuring."

"Actually, it's not that likely," John interjected. "Given that the gene seems to only develop in the presence of a Lycan true mate, and given we mostly keep to within the packs, the chances of unknowing dormants running into their mate and thus triggering their latent side seems unlikely."

"Say that to Bailey," Wyatt wryly replied. "Okay, so we can all agree we've been wrong about dormants, fine. The more serious problems at hand is how Roderick knew and why he wants Bailey."

As usual, Wyatt bluntly went to the heart of the problem, and Gavin didn't like the look of it. "Did he know or suspect? Don't forget, they took all her mother's information the night they abducted her. So while Roderick or his minions might have suspected something special about her, they couldn't know for sure until they did more background."

"Given their ardent pursuit of her, I think it's safe to say they now know what she is. We need to get this information out to the other packs immediately," Nathan ordered. "Tell them to start sifting through their records and start contacting all dormants who've left the packs, and have their children either brought in or put under observation."

"I'll get started on our own records," John volunteered.

"What do you want us to do?" Gavin asked.

"For now, you and Wyatt should keep a close eye on your mate because my gut says Roderick's not done with her."

Funny, because Gavin's intuition said the same thing.

Chapter Fourteen

Falling into an enjoyable routine proved surprisingly easy, and Bailey couldn't recall ever feeling this content. Then again, she'd never had four men striving to please her at every turn.

Already more than a week here and she couldn't imagine life without any of them. But that still didn't mean she'd jumped into bonding with Parker and Jaxon just yet. With Gavin and Wyatt, it had just kind of naturally happened. However, while Parker and Jaxon stole quite a few kisses—to her panty-wetting enjoyment—interruptions and distraction kept things from going any further, and she was too shy to claim them directly.

At least they didn't seem to mind the wait, even if they did tease her all the time. Perhaps, if the lusts they roused weren't being satisfied nightly by Wyatt or Gavin—sometimes with both men at once—she might have given them what they so blatantly desired. Truth was, though, she liked things the way they were, and she didn't want to rock the boat or create cause for jealousy, despite their reassurances this was the pack way.

It was Dana who inadvertently made Bailey see that she needed to perhaps step up her game and claim her men before someone else did.

They were strolling through the compound when Dana bristled beside her. Bailey looked around to see what had caught her attention but only saw a man leaving a house, a self-satisfied smirk on his face.

"What's wrong?" she asked.

"Damned slut," Dana muttered. "It's not enough she's got four mates working their asses off to give her shit she doesn't need. She's now seducing some of the single men into giving her more."

Bailey's brow wrinkled. "Why on earth would she do that? I have a hard enough time keeping up with two."

"Her men don't work within the compound. They're truckers, and to make the kind of money she likes, they do long haul. Most women time it so that there's always one at home to keep her company. Not Missy. She spreads her legs to give them a taste and then sends them off again. Hell, the door's barely slammed shut before she's got some young pup in there, rutting his brains out."

"Okay, that's just wrong," Bailey replied, making a moue of distaste.

"Yup, but there's no pack laws against fucking," Dana said crudely, "which is why you'd better make up your mind on what you're going to do with Jaxon and Parker. I hear Missy's got her eye on them. And she's not the only one. Some of the newcomers are single women looking for some men that they haven't known since childhood to settle with. With the disappearances of males from all over, we've also got some females looking to pad their families with as many men as they can get their paws on for added protection. Prime specimens like Parker and Jaxon won't stay single for long."

"But they're mine," Bailey blurted out, almost immediately blushing.

Dana snorted. "Not until you bite them, they're not. And even then, they can stray. My father wasn't one to keep it in his pants."

Bailey bit her lip. "You think they'll cheat on me?"

Dana whirled and grabbed her hands. "Oh shit, I didn't mean your men would. Anyone can tell they're nuts for you. You have a true mating bond with them just like I do with my guys. But not all women have that. Some just mate because it's convenient or they're lonely. Those are the ones that don't tend to have happily ever afters."

"And are Jaxon and Parker my true mates too?"

"I'd say yes, but until you mark them, they're also fair game. Keep in mind, the bond only needs an exchange of blood, whether freely given or not. It's not unheard of for a man, or woman, for that matter, to trick someone. It's unethical, but it still happens. It's partially why we had the laws restructured, to eradicate that kind of behavior. But once bound, there's nothing short of death that can break that circle."

Before Bailey could question her further, a commotion caught their attention. One of Dana's mates approached with their son. The little bundle of energy tore away from John's hand and ran up the street, his little legs pumping.

"Mama!" he bellowed.

Dana scooped the boy up and whirled him about to his chortling glee. At just under two years of age, Braedon was the spitting image of his father, John.

"What happened to his nap?" she asked, settling her son on her hip.

Reaching them, Dana's mate shrugged helplessly. "Yeah, that didn't work out so well. I was hoping a walk would calm him down."

"Not likely," she grumbled, but her fierce expression melted as her son kissed her wetly on the cheek with a loud smacking sound.

Looking upon them created a longing for a family of her own. A child, our child. *Now that I'm Lycan like them, will I be able to have children? Could I already be pregnant?*

As Dana made Braedon wave good-bye and left to put him down for an actual nap, Bailey couldn't help watching them wistfully.

As if reading her mind, John said, "You'll be blessed like that as well soon."

"You think?"

"When was your last period?"

Bailey turned red at his blunt question. Doctor to the compound or not, outside in a social setting, such an intimate query rattled her. "I don't know. A week or so before I met Gavin and the others."

"And that was about two weeks or so ago, almost three, right?"

She nodded.

"It's probably too early to tell, although I'm sure they've been diligent about their duty. If you'd like, though, I could drop by a few testers so you can check for yourself without the hassle of coming to my office."

"Could you?"

"Yes. I'll have my secretary bring them around. They're fairly standard. Pee on the stick. A cross is yes. A minus is no."

"What if I am? Will they be happy, though?" She wondered if it had even occurred to her men that their copious lovemaking without protection might result in pregnancy. She sure hadn't until this moment. If she already were with child, how would they react?

John's knowing eyes saw through her trepidation, and he replied softly, "All pregnancies are celebrated in the pack. Girl or boy, no one is ever upset when a mating is successful. Knowing Gavin and Wyatt, they will strut around like proud peacocks if their seed has already taken root."

Bailey pondered her conversation with John and Dana for a few days, masking her thought process behind bright smiles that seemed to fool them. Well, except for Wyatt. He watched her with those dark eyes of his and even questioned if anything bothered her. She evaded replying with an impromptu seduction that left him barely able to say her name.

During that time of reflection, she made her decision to take Parker as mate. Given all the time he'd patiently taken to teach her how to use her new abilities and to defend herself, sparring lessons that left her rubbing her posterior on more than one occasion, she felt he'd earned the right to go next. Besides, she was tired of fighting her attraction to him. Maybe once she claimed him, the wolf in her head, whose presence no longer freaked her out as much, would stop her bitching.

Of course, she would make up her mind on the worst possible day, the day Parker wanted her to coax her beast out.

Bailey crossed her arms over her chest and shook her head stubbornly. "No."

Parker sighed. "Baby, I've taught you everything else. It's the only thing left. Come on, do it with me now. It will be easier if you're the one allowing it rather than waiting for the next full moon to force it."

"Can't we do something else instead?"

"Like what? I've stalled this for far longer than I should have already."

Now is my chance. She'd never initiated the kisses before, but there was no time like the present. Smiling coyly, Bailey sauntered up to Parker until she stood just a hairsbreadth away from his chest. A trembling invaded her limbs as she lifted her hands and placed them on his chest. Her new hearing caught the increase in his heart rate, a sign that encouraged her to lift on tiptoe and tilt her head back.

"I'm sure we can think of something to do," she said huskily.

If the smoky desire in his gaze was any indication, he'd caught her innuendo. "We're kind of exposed out here."

"Out here" being still within sight of the housing units that bordered the woods kept within the compound boundaries. "Well then, let's go find something a little more private," she sassed before sprinting off with a giggle.

Behind her, Parker let out a howl that even in his man shape sounded animalistic, and the chase began. Bailey ran through the woods, nimble as a jackrabbit—or in this case, a wolf—leaping over debris, faster than she'd imagined herself capable. All the exercise with Parker had an added benefit. Even in the short time she'd been here, she'd noticed a change in her body, a tightening of her muscles that secretly made her smile. Sure, she'd probably always own wide hips and a set of boobs that needed a bra to harness them, but her arms and legs had lost their flabby look. *And I feel great!*

The crashing of Parker behind her, his way of letting her know he still followed, made her grin. Anticipation built in her as she imagined him catching her, and she knew just the place too—the farthest corner of the compound, where a natural glade with a bed of the softest grass awaited.

As soon as she hit the hidden paradise, she stopped and whirled, in time to see Parker leap out after her. His chest heaved, not with exertion but an attempt at control if the passion in his eyes was any indication. Panting slightly herself, Bailey didn't say a word but let her hands stray to the buttons on her blouse, slipping each one out of its loop until her shirt came loose. Shrugging it from her shoulders, she let it flutter to the ground and stood there, trying not to blush at her brazenness, but failing. Wyatt and Gavin had done a lot in the last few weeks to give her the confidence she needed in her own body to feel sexy.

"Oh, baby, you are so beautiful." He breathed the words with a reverence that made her shiver.

Parker stripped off his own shirt as he stalked toward her, revealing slabs of muscle that made her breath hitch. He stopped a few feet from her, and eyes locked to his, Bailey reached to her waist and pushed down the yoga pants she'd worn for their session. They pooled around her ankles, and she stepped out of them.

Then, before she could lose her nerve, she removed her bra and panties as well.

Naked, she didn't have a chance to shiver, or second-guess her decision, because Parker swept her up into a hug that lifted her feet off the ground and brought her mouth level with his. The heat of his embrace burned and ignited her own raging desire. His embraces of before were nothing compared to the hunger he displayed now—a hunger reciprocated.

Her own need unleashed, she returned his kiss just as fiercely, her tongue boldly pressing against his lips until he opened for her, allowing exploration. The deep groan that rumbled from him made his whole chest vibrate, making her own body hum. Somehow, holding on to her the entire while, he sat them down, and then he lay down at her urging so she could plaster herself against his length.

But there was one thing he'd forgotten, and she kept encountering it every time she rubbed her cleft against him.

Sitting up, she straddled his waist and reached behind to unsnap his pants, needing to feel him inside her, skin to skin. A flash of reflected light caught her attention, and she froze mid-motion, staring. Yellow eyes, with irises of deep red, regarded her from the shadows of the trees.

Sensing something amiss, Parker opened his eyes. "What is it, baby?" He'd no sooner asked than he stiffened beneath her. In a flash, he'd rolled and gotten up on one knee, placing her behind him.

"When I say go," he murmured in a low voice, "run as fast as you can back to the compound. Tell the others the rogues have crossed the wall."

Rogues? Here? Instant fear washed over her, a fear

that trebled as more sets of eyes appeared beside the first then advanced.

"Get ready, baby," Parker said, standing to his full height. "Go!" He shouted the word just as his body began to morph, his pants splitting at the violent change and then falling away as his legs took on the slimmer shape of a wolf's. And just in time, too, because he'd no sooner finished shifting than the renegade wolves leapt at him.

Frozen, Bailey could only watch in horror as four wolves dove and snapped at Parker. Tears came to her eyes at the first bloody gash, but while Bailey, the human, shook, her inner beast trembled in fury. She whined in her head, begging to get out so she could help their mate.

But it will hurt, whined her cowardly side.

And Parker might die, if we don't, retorted her inner bitch. Her mental battle took only seconds, but it was long enough for one of the rogues to notice she still stood there, naked as a jaybird and defenseless.

When it took a step in her direction, Bailey relinquished control. *Fine. Change. But do it fast before they kill him.* Her wolf wasted no time, bounding forward in her mind, taking over her body and pushing herself through.

A scream left Bailey's lips as her body convulsed and contorted, but the agony either didn't last as long or wasn't as bad as she remembered because, in no time at all, she was howling instead, her wolf gleefully in charge and advancing on the rogue.

They met in a heavy clash of bodies that made the old Bailey want to cower but made the new one thirst for blood. And vengeance.

Because of this Lycan prick, and others, she'd been abducted, hunted, and terrified. No more. It stopped now.

I'm done hiding and being frightened. It's time they learned to leave me alone. That I will not give up without a fight.

She just wished the path to tranquility wasn't so bloody. Eeew.

* * * *

Parker couldn't believe it when Bailey stayed and finally embraced her beast. Even more amazing, she remained to fight alongside him. Not that he needed her aid, but he'd never tell her that, not given the courage she displayed with her actions.

Pride made him howl as he took out the rogues who'd interrupted their mating tryst. Stupid, ill-timed bastards. Another fifteen minutes, tops, and he would have claimed Bailey as his own.

More annoying, once he took care of these upstarts, he'd have to go back to warn Gavin, Nathan, and the others, his chance to resume where they'd left off irrevocably lost. It made him vicious, and in short order, he and Bailey were the only wolves standing.

Parker called up his human half, but when he

looked at Bailey—her coat a curly black like her hair—she whined.

"Poor baby. Is your wolf not ready to go back in its cage? I warned you this would happen."

A chuckle he couldn't help made her glare at him and bare some teeth. It made him laugh harder, her cuteness always multiplying when she got riled. A shift in the wind made Parker lift his head to sniff audibly. "Looks like the cavalry is about to arrive."

A six-pack of wolves burst into the clearing, Gavin vying with Nathan for the lead. In moments, Gavin stood before him, along with Nathan, surveying the bloody remains.

"He dares send rogues inside my compound!" Nathan's low roar vibrated with power, an alpha trait that made Parker's ears ache. "Fan out. Search these woods. I want to know if there are more of them. And if you find some, bring me one alive." Nathan's body heaved with repressed fury as he clenched at his sides.

"What about Bailey?" Parker asked.

Gavin answered him from his knees as he stroked her, nuzzling her face with his own while Wyatt, still in his wolf shape, paced alongside. "Take her back to the house and guard her." His friend then winked. "Good job getting her to go furry. I don't envy being in your shoes, though, when she turns back."

Judging by Bailey's drooping ears, she didn't either. Parker quickly dressed in his tattered pants, not one to walk around nude unless it was necessary, although given the gaping rents, he had to wonder if he showed more than he hid.

The wolves, who'd arrived too late for battle, took off again, Wyatt in the lead, except for Nathan and Gavin, who knelt by the bodies to examine them further.

Seeing no need for them to remain any further, Parker left, long strides taking him into the woods. Bailey trotted alongside him. Despite her current form, he still spoke to her as if she would answer.

"That was a real brave thing you did back here, baby. But I'll tell you it just about scared the life out of me."

A snuffling noise came from her wolf.

"Yeah, scoff all you want. When I wanted you to embrace your wolf, I meant as a part of you, not so you could put yourself in danger. It's our job to protect you."

That earned him a sideways glare.

Parker chuckled. "What am I going to do with you, baby? You are so bloody cute and stubborn. I sure wish we hadn't gotten interrupted. I was sure looking forward to sinking into your sweet little body and having you claim me as mate."

Her head butted his hand, and he stroked her between the ears.

"I take it you're kind of sad too. Well, there's probably still enough time before the others get back from the search of the woods. That is if you can figure out how to swap shapes again. Or are you going to wait until your wolf does that for you again too?" He threw the taunt intentionally and waited.

Sure enough, she stopped in her tracks and, with a mournful howl, switched bodies. She remained on her hands and knees for a moment, panting, the pain of her change slowly receding, before raising her face to fix him with a triumphant smirk.

"Ha! See? I can do it. I just choose not to."

And with those saucy words, she stood and began to walk away then stopped dead, her head cocked in thought. Parker caught up, scooped her up, and continued walking.

She struggled in his grasp. "Put me down. We need a plan."

"A plan for what?" he asked, distracted by the soft, naked curves in his arms.

"We can't go back like this!"

"But I like you like this," he retorted, squeezing her to his nude chest. A good thing he'd taken the time to put on his pants, even if they were somewhat splattered with blood, and holey, else he'd be striding along with a hard-on in full view. Actually, given the broken zipper, chances were something showed.

It delighted him that she still blushed. "I'm sure you do like me like this, but you can't just go walking into the village with me naked in your arms."

"Why not?"

A heavy sigh escaped her. "Because I'm naked."

"Trust me. No one will bat an eye. Lycans, remember? Nudity is a common sight around here. Sometimes our clothes don't survive a sudden transition. Or we change from our wolves to our fleshy selves while still in the woods. Now, if you were to arrive, though, wearing a bush or some leaves like some kind of forest nymph, that would get you noticed."

"I really hate arguing with you guys."

"Then don't," he replied with a grin. "Did I forget to mention wolves are stubborn?"

She just snorted again and then buried her face in his chest, not lifting it until they'd made it inside their house safely. He brought her straight into the bathroom with its large stall shower.

Parker let her slide down his body slowly, loving the sensual friction of her soft skin against his. Leaning around her, he turned on the tap, letting the water warm up. Her small hands went to his pants, tugged down the ruined fabric, and Parker swallowed hard as his cock sprang forth, ready and thick for her.

"You know, when I read 'Little Red Riding Hood' as a little girl, I never expected one day I'd have the chance to say, 'My what a big cock you have,'" she murmured, stroking his length with the tip of one finger.

His reply emerged hoarse. "All the better to love you with."

"Do you?" she asked, raising her gaze.

He cupped her face with his hands. "More and more each day."

A smile spread across her face, and he caught a hint of moisture in her eyes. "I love you too."

"Oh, baby." He forwent words to lift her up and crush her mouth against his. Despite the strength of his hug, she didn't flinch from his passion and embraced him back with an urgency that awed him. He stepped into the shower with her, his hands still spanning her waist, and he dunked them under the needling spray.

The cascading water sluiced down their bodies, washing the grime of their adventure away, but even better, it left them slippery. The slide of skin against skin made Parker rumble with pleasure, but he wanted more than a sensual tease. He set her down and then dropped to his knees before her, a supplicant looking to worship the haven of her flesh. Angling one of her thighs over his shoulder, he exposed her glistening cleft to his view, and she steadied herself by digging her fingers into his scalp. Then he found nirvana.

Leaning forward, he swiped his tongue across her, loving how she shuddered and a moan vibrated through her body. He licked again and again, unable to resist the taste of her. She shivered against the wall, her panting cries urging him on. He thrust a blunt finger into her sex while he plied her clit, and his cock jerked at her response. Her pussy clung to his digit tightly, the wet suction a precursor for what he'd feel when he sank into her.

Above him she gasped and made her demand clear. "Bite me. Claim me, Parker."

Her sweet plea nearly undid him, and he buried his face against her thigh for a moment to control himself.

Her fingers stroked gently across his scalp.

"Make me yours, Parker. Please."

Only a foolish man would deny her request, and he was anything but a fool. He kissed the smooth skin of her thigh before opening his mouth wide. His wolf was ready, dropping down his incisors and sinking them into her flesh, claiming her. She keened, her hips thrusting forth as he sucked at the blood that oozed from his mating wound. He took just enough for the ritual then stood. When he would have lifted her to plow her sex, she surprised him. Dropping to her knees, she grasped him and shot him a sultry smile before bending her head.

Parker let out a hoarse shout as she took the head of his cock into her mouth, sucking at him, drawing him deep and suctioning tightly. He fisted a hand in her hair, unable to resist guiding her motion, setting them into a rhythm that had his balls tightening and his cock swelling almost painfully.

"Now," he whispered. "Oh God, baby. Take me now before I lose it."

With a final wet suck, she released him and latched onto his thigh, biting into the flesh, drawing his essence into her mouth. Parker roared as the binding completed between them with an almost thunderous clap.

Dazed, but still hard and needing to feel her flesh around him, he manhandled her until she bent over in front of him, her delectable bottom pushed up and spread. He couldn't help running a hand down her silken slit, and she shuddered.

"Now. Take me now, Parker. Oh God, I need you."

They were the sweetest words he'd ever heard moaned. Parker speared her with his length, a firm thrust that seated him inside her and made her cry out. The flesh of her channel squeezed around him, and Parker's head went back at the blissful feel of her. Hands on her hips, he began to pump, sheathing himself in and out of her, the juices of her passion easing his passage, even though her muscles kept tightening convulsively around him. The curve of her buttocks slammed nicely back into his groin as he took her in the way he'd dreamed of so many sleepless nights. Of course, his imagination hadn't done justice to the reality.

A ripple went through her as he continued to seesaw into her welcoming flesh. She screamed as her orgasm shook her, the tremors of it fisting him in tumultuous waves. With a bellow, Parker shot his seed into her, his body arched and his head thrown back. He held his position, deeply seated within her, until the shaking subsided. He never wanted to leave, but it wasn't just about his wants and needs, not anymore. Still panting, and awestruck, he let his dick slip from her, and he pulled upright so he could hold her cradled against his chest.

"I love you, Bailey," he murmured, his heart so full of this woman.

"My Parker, my mate," she replied possessively, hugging him tight. "Thank you."

A chuckle made his chest rumble as they stood in the pouring water of the shower. *Only my sweet baby would thank me after the gift she bestowed upon me.* He loved her even more.

Chapter Fifteen

Nervousness made her pace and gnaw at her nails while Parker, a content look on his face and his eyes hooded, watched her from his position on the couch.

"They're going to be fine," he reiterated.

Still, she worried. While she and her newest mate had returned more than two hours ago, made love twice, and even eaten, they'd yet to hear word on the others. Fear over their safety comprised part of her anxiety, but the other part of her angst she blamed on fear. She'd claimed Parker, her gentle giant, but how would Wyatt and Gavin react? And Jaxon, would he get angry at being the only one left?

The raucous noise of their return preceded their entrance into the house, Jaxon leading the cacophony with his usual humor. Gavin strode over to her and kissed her first, followed by Wyatt. Then Jaxon tried to sneak a smooch but ended up tripped by Gavin and missing. Covering her mouth lest she laugh at his chagrin, she then watched wide-eyed as her first two mates went over and shook Parker's hand.

"Congrats, brother. About time she made up her mind," Gavin said.

"Well, we already knew she had good taste when she chose me," Wyatt replied.

Bailey shook her head, not quite sure how they'd guessed without her telling, but then again, it was hard to miss the satisfaction evident on Parker's face. Sneaking a glance at Jaxon, she noted he didn't appear angry or hurt, just wistful, a fleeting look that disappeared under a lopsided grin.

"So what's for dinner? Other than pie," he added with a lascivious wink that made her blush and her lovers bristle.

As they all sat down to eat some leftovers slapped into sandwiches, Bailey listened avidly as the boys caught her up on the hunt. It seemed the rogues had penetrated in two areas. She and Parker had taken care of one invasion while several squads of wolves tracked down the other set that had escaped and took care of them.

Not satisfied, Nathan made the squads of Lycans do another sweep of the compound and the surrounding area, looking for evidence of more. Despite finding nothing, Nathan ordered increased round-the-clock patrols of the perimeter and was bumping up the number of guards walking the boundary from two to four.

Unease made Bailey toy with her food, but no one called her on it. When the others cleared the table, Wyatt stayed behind and fixed her with his dark gaze.

"What's up, sunshine?"

Dropping her gaze, she traced the wooden grain of the tabletop. "Nothing," she muttered.

She heard his chair go sliding back on the floor with a screech, and a moment later, he knelt at her side, peering up at her. "Don't lie to me."

"This is because of me," she whispered.

"What makes you think that?"

"I'm not stupid. Even I can make the connection. Rogues keep coming after me. Roderick controls them. It's obvious he wants me. Heck, he wants me bad enough he's attacking the compound. And he's not going to stop until he gets me."

Wyatt dragged her off the chair and snuggled her in his lap, his arms banded around her.

"Never. He's never going to get his hands on you. Do you understand me? I will protect you with my life before I allow that. We all will."

"But what if he keeps coming? People are going to get hurt."

"Not if we take care of Roderick first."

"What are you saying? Are you planning something?" She peppered him with frantic questions, but Wyatt didn't answer further, despite how much she prodded.

The next few days, everyone acted like nothing was the matter, but she could feel an undercurrent around her. Her lessons with Parker continued but changed to a safer locale, the forest deemed off-limits to everyone until the rogue situation got resolved. Fear hung heavily in the air. The men never came out and said she was in danger, but she noticed how they did their best to keep her within the main part of the compound—and never left her alone. Worse, they kept secrets. And the subterfuge didn't just involve her men. Even Dana could only shrug when Bailey questioned her on what was afoot.

The only conclusion to draw from the avoidance of her questions, and the whispers out of hearing, was that they didn't trust her. Knowing how little they thought of her depressed and upset her, which, in turn, made her sick to her stomach. She started to dream, if you could call the nightmares she woke from shaking and sweaty something so gentle. She couldn't recall what had terrified her so when she woke whimpering or crying, and each time, one of her three lovers would hold her in his arms and croon softly to her until she fell back asleep.

Despite their attempts at normalcy and their evident affection, she withdrew into herself. But only for so long before frustration made her snap.

She confronted Gavin a week after the attack, unable to handle it anymore. "What's going on?"

A shuttered look came over his face. "Nothing."

The lie hit her like a kick to the stomach. "You don't trust me, do you?" she accused.

"Of course I trust you," he replied, but he didn't look her in the eye when he said it, his taut frame reinforcing the lie. She whirled to run from him, tears flooding her eyes.

He caught her and spun her back into his chest. "Darling, please. I trust *you*. I do, but remember those five days you lost, the ones you can't recall?"

She sniffed against his chest and nodded.

"Nathan's afraid—actually, we're all concerned—that Roderick might have done something to you. Planted some kind of seed or ability to spy in your mind."

The words took a moment to filter. "You think I'm going to betray you?" Bailey pushed away and gaped at him, hurt. "I would never do anything to hurt you or anyone else here. How could you think that?"

"I know *you* wouldn't. But Roderick is one truly evil bastard. I wouldn't put it past him to have done something to you."

"So you're all waiting for me to go off? Is that it? What do you think I'm going to do? Go postal and shoot you all in your sleep?"

"I don't know, which is why we need to be careful. I don't want to keep secrets, darling, really I don't, but don't you see? By not telling you anything, you can't betray us, even if it's unintentionally."

"So, what, I'm going to be an outsider for the rest of my life? Treated like some prisoner?" Her voice broke. Gavin tried to draw her back into his arms, but she stepped out of reach.

A frustrated sigh blew out of him, and he ran a hand through his hair. "Of course not. This is temporary. Just until we take care of Roderick once and for all." His words were an eerie echo of Wyatt's.

"Oh my God. You're going after the psycho."

"We can't. We have no idea where he is."

But she'd heard enough. Despite everything they'd shared, and the love he claimed, he didn't trust her. He thought she'd betray the pack. *And the worst part is he's probably right.* She still couldn't recall those five missing days.

With a strangled cry, she fled, ignoring his plea to come back. She locked herself in the bedroom they'd given her and cried. It didn't matter they probably knew better than her what Roderick was capable of. It didn't matter they'd not let up in their attentions or affection to her. The fact that they could even think that her subconscious harbored a bomb or, worse, that someone watched her actions through her mind made her sick.

Red eyes bored into hers while a slick voice murmured incomprehensible words. She pulled against the chains . . .

Bailey lurched off the bed, ran for the bathroom, and spewed her lunch into the porcelain bowl. Slumping beside it, drained emotionally and physically, she could only shake.

What was that I saw?

This wasn't the first time she'd experienced an odd flashback, and she sobbed anew as she realized what it probably meant. She did hide something awful in her mind—something that could hurt everyone she'd come to care for.

Crawling out to the bedroom, she made it back onto the bed, where she hugged herself, rocking her body and ignoring the knocks on the door. Hours passed, and she thought they'd all forgotten her until she heard a metallic ping at the door. With a click, the door opened, and Jaxon sauntered in balancing a tray.

"Go away," she muttered. "Don't you know I'm dangerous?"

"Sure, tempt me, why don't you? I live for danger," he exclaimed with a bright smile, setting down the tray on the comforter before flopping onto the end of the bed.

He snagged a fry off the plate he uncovered, the aroma of the food making her stomach churn unhappily.

"I'm not hungry," she said, her tone sulky.

"What? And here I went through all this trouble."

"Fries and chicken nuggets with canned corn is trouble?" she replied wryly.

"I'll have you know that can opener is finicky."

"You are such a ham."

"I prefer dog," he replied seriously before lolling his tongue and panting.

Bailey giggled. She couldn't help it. Jaxon seemed bound and determined to make her smile, and as usual, he succeeded. She grabbed a fry to chew on to make him happy. No sooner did she swallow than she ran for the bathroom, gagging.

A hand stroked her spine while she heaved, and when she stood weakly, Jaxon scooped her into his arms to carry her back to bed. After settling her, he disposed of the tray and climbed in beside her, propping his head on one hand to regard her.

"So who's the daddy do you think?"

At first, her brain didn't comprehend. When it did, the pieces fell together: her moodiness, tears, and now the throwing up.

She staggered out of the bed and into the bathroom. Dropping to her knees, she then opened the cabinet and rifled through the contents.

"I know I hid it in here somewhere," she muttered under her breath, feeling so stupid for not thinking of the reason for her malaise.

"What did you hide? *Playboy* magazines? A vibrator?"

"No. This!" She held up the paper bag triumphantly, and when Jaxon raised a brow, she shooed him out of the bathroom instead of answering. She tore open the package and pulled out the slim wand with its little window.

Dropping her pants first, she inelegantly squatted over the toilet and forced a stream of pee out. She hit her hand first before soaking the stick. Grossed out, she put the pregnancy wand on the counter, wiped, and then washed her hands. She kept her eyes peeled on the little square as she scrubbed.

A cross appeared.

"Holy cow, I'm pregnant." Oddly, the realization

relieved her instead of sending her into a full-blown breakdown. Pregnancy would explain so much, including why she'd acted like a psycho manic bitch all week long.

Grabbing the proof, she flung the door open and said, "Jaxon, get the boys. I need to tell them something."

Picking food off her tray, Jaxon tossed a, "They're out patrolling and won't be back for hours," over his shoulder.

"Oh."

He rolled, still chewing, to face her. "Why? What's up, sweet cheeks? You look like you're going to burst."

She waved the stick at him. "I'm not some crazy emotional bitch. I'm pregnant."

A blank look dropped over Jaxon's face. "Pregnant?"

For a moment, red eyes flashed in front of Bailey, a vision gone when she blinked. "Do you think the boys will be happy?" she asked, suddenly uncertain, as Jaxon sprang up off the bed.

He stalked toward her, not saying a word, a grimace contorting his face, and his eyes . . . Dear God, the irises in his eyes were red.

Bailey backed away from him. "Jaxon?" Her voice wavered.

For a moment, a look of horror flashed over his face, but his hands still stretched toward her. "Run, Bailey," he gasped. "I can't stop him."

She waited a half second too long. Jaxon grabbed her, and though she struggled, she couldn't escape. A blow to the side of her head sank her into darkness.

* * * *

"I can't wait until we take care of Roderick. I can't stand seeing her so miserable," Wyatt grumbled, feeling like a useless idiot bumbling in the darkness looking for rogues who had, once again, vanished without a trace.

"Tell me about it. The whole mating bond means I feel how sad and uneasy she is all the time. It's not fair. I can't believe she'd do something to betray us," Parker added.

"Not her, Roderick. I hate it as much as you guys, but I get the feeling it won't be long now. Nathan is convinced the bastard is hiding close by, and given the way he keeps jabbing at our defenses, I agree."

"But where?" Wyatt griped. His frustration got the better of him, and he punched the trunk of a tree, splintering the bark.

"He's got balls, that's for fucking sure."

"And wolves to waste," Parker added.

They lapsed into silence after that, letting themselves sink into their own thoughts as they waded through brush and bramble looking for a sign rogues had passed this way.

The fear, sharp and sudden, came through his link with Bailey loud and clear, and then nothing. Stopping abruptly, Wyatt turned to face Gavin and Parker, who searched the forest outside the compound with him.

"Did you feel that?"

They didn't answer, instead taking off running, back toward their SUV, but they'd wandered far from the road in their grid search, and it took an eternity to make it to their vehicle. Parker took the wheel, spinning the tires in his haste to return.

It seemed crazy to think someone or something had penetrated so deep into pack to get to Bailey, especially given the crazy security around the place. However, rationalization couldn't overcome his trepidation, and he especially didn't like the way his link to her refused to respond.

When they arrived at the compound gates, pandemonium reigned, with the on-guard duty knocked out cold, drugged, apparently, and unable to answer questions. Still not speaking, Wyatt and his pack brothers raced to the house. He already knew she was gone, but he searched the place anyway, frantically calling her name.

She didn't reply, and they discovered another chilling fact. Jaxon appeared gone as well.

Spilling back out onto the street, they ran into Nathan, grim-faced as usual, Dana at his side, her face a mask of anger.

"We were watching the wrong wolf," she spat.

"What do you mean?" Wyatt asked.

Nathan growled. "All this time, we assumed Bailey was the ticking time bomb, but it was never her. She was the objective. Jaxon was the means to get her."

"Jaxon betrayed the pack? I don't believe it," Parker said shaking his head.

"I doubt it's what he wanted," Dana said. "But somehow, Roderick got to him and invaded his mind."

"But why now? What happened to make him go off?" Gavin exclaimed, his face haggard and his voice drawn.

Wyatt straightened. "Shit. Hold on a second." Racing back into the house, he flew to the bathroom and grabbed the packaging from the counter that he'd ignored before. His stomach fell as his suspicion proved true. It was with sluggish steps that he returned and held up the reason for her abduction.

"She's pregnant?" Gavin's brows arched.

"That was the trigger, I'll bet," Wyatt said.

"Oh fuck," Dana exclaimed in a most unladylike manner.

"We need to get her back," Nathan intoned.

"And how do you propose that? It's not like Roderick left a map to his location, and we've yet to find any clue as to his hideout," Wyatt drawled sarcastically, not caring if he was being rude to his leader. Frustration made him want to yell worse.

A grim smile ghosted across Nathan's face. "Actually, we do have a map. I took the liberty of chipping your mate."

Dana dropped her eyes. "I've been feeding it to her in muffins for the last few days."

"And you didn't tell us?" Gavin bristled while Wyatt fought an urge to let his wolf make mincemeat out of the people he trusted.

"Only Dana, myself, and John knew. We didn't want to take the risk someone else would slip and let Roderick know."

"You wanted him to take her," Wyatt spat, realization setting in.

Nathan's face darkened. "Not wanted. Expected. And, I might add, it's a good thing I did, or our chances of getting her back would be slim to none. Now, would you like to keep standing around debating the decision I made, or are we assembling the pack to get her back?"

"Let's go kick some ass," Gavin said, his eyes narrowing with menace.

"And bash some skulls," Parker added, flexing his meaty fists.

"Time to shed some blood." Wyatt's cold tone brought a smile to their faces, the lupine smile of a predator about to go on a hunt. *Time to kill.*

Chapter Sixteen

Opening her eyes, Bailey blinked in the dim light, staring at the cracked cement ceiling. Why did it seem so familiar?

A clawed hand drags sharply across my skin. Blood beads, dripping down. He laughs, drawing near with his damned needles and his hungry mouth.

Shaking her head, she tried to dislodge the memories, but faster than a speeding bullet, they filled her mind, the echoes of her past screams ringing in her head, ricocheting off the horrifying recollections that wouldn't stop coming. The cries, the screams, the blood, so much blood, and *him*. Roderick.

Clutching at her aching skull, she rocked back and forth, but she couldn't stop the tears, the horror. *He tortured me.* Too much to take all at once, she sank into oblivion.

Wakening a second time, Bailey moaned as she recognized the nightmarish décor around her. *I'm back.*

She recalled most of those forgotten days, horrific days that seemed a lifetime ago, recalled Roderick as he laughed at her misery and then gleefully applied more. She didn't remember everything he'd said, the pain controlling too much of her conscious thought, but she did remember one phrase in particular, and even now, it made her shiver.

"You shall be the mother of my army. With your womb, I shall rule the packs."

A moan slipped from her, and she stifled it as she heard a rustle.

"Bailey?" The uncertain voice made her eyes pop open.

Jaxon, looking worn and dejected, knelt before her.

"You!" She spat the word at him as she scrambled back. "How could you do this?"

"Bailey—I—"

The misery in his eyes hurt her, which she didn't understand. The traitor didn't deserve any sympathy, not after hand-delivering her to the monster.

"You betrayed your pack, Jaxon. Betrayed me," she cried, watching as he flinched at each of her thrown words.

"I didn't want to," he moaned. "He got in my head. I had no choice. He controlled me. Oh God, I wish Wyatt had killed me like he kept threatening. I should have died that night in the park."

"The night I attacked you?"

He nodded. "Once Wyatt left to look for you, Roderick came out of the darkness. I tried to fight. I really did. But I was too weak, and he got into my head." He grimaced in remembered pain.

"Oh, Jaxon." Her tone softened. She knew all too well what Roderick was capable of.

"I didn't even remember until I woke up in this cell," he admitted with a mournful sigh. "I wondered why I kept dreaming of red eyes. I swear I didn't know what he did to me. As soon as you said 'pregnant,' I wasn't me anymore. It was like I was a passenger while he drove. And he'd had me stash things, like drugs to knock you and the guards at the gate out." His shoulders shook as his head dropped to hide his tears of shame. "I wish I'd known. I would have killed myself before I hurt you or the pack," he whispered.

Sliding over to him, she put her arm around his shaking shoulders. "I know, Jaxon. He hurt me too. And then made me forget."

"What does he want?"

She placed her free hand on her stomach. "He wants my child."

"But why?"

"Because he thinks my child is the key for him to build an army to destroy the packs."

"That makes no sense."

"I know, but don't forget, Roderick isn't all there."

"Tell me about it. I thought Wyatt was the coldest killer I know. This guy makes him look like a docile bunny rabbit."

"How long have we been here?"

"I don't know. At least a day. Maybe more. I

remember driving for a long time before we got here."

"Wherever we are, we need to get out."

Jaxon sprang up and went to the door, which of course didn't budge when he yanked on it. He pounded on it before she could stop him, the metallic echo dying slowly until silence reigned, the gabbling madness and despair of those imprisoned from her last tenure missing. Perhaps death had come to rescue them.

"Save your strength," she cautioned. "We'll need to wait until he opens the door before we can make our move."

Resigned, Jaxon leaned against a cement wall and slid down. His body posture screamed he wanted her to leave him alone. She ignored it and sidled over until she sat beside him. He flinched when she laid her head on his shoulder.

"You know, I had your claiming all planned," she said softly.

"Y-You did?" His voice emerged hesitant, so unlike the brash Jaxon she knew. It broke her heart.

"Yup. I was going to bake a coconut cream pie."

"My favorite."

"I know. I figured you'd end up making some smart-ass remark, and I was going to throw my portion in your face."

A rusty chuckle made him shake. "What a waste of pie."

"Not really, because in my plan, you threw yours

right back. And then"—she turned her head until she whispered against his ear—"I was going to lick it off you."

"You are a wicked girl, sweet cheeks," he said, turning until their lips hovered a hairsbreadth apart.

"I've been learning from the best," she said, letting herself lean in that last millimeter to touch his mouth.

Their kiss was slow, sensual, and bittersweet. They both knew their chances of making it out of there lingered in the slim-to-fat-chance realm. It made tears prick her eyes to know that she'd waited too long to claim this wonderful man. She deepened the kiss when she heard the sound of steps approaching. Just as desperate, he clung to her, and when she bit his lip, she hoped he got the hint as the flavor of his blood hit her tongue. He managed to nip her back just inside the lip before the door burst open. They both opened their eyes wide as the shock wave of their joining hit.

"Isn't this cozy?" sneered a familiar gravelly voice.

Bailey turned from Jaxon to peer upon the face of her nightmare. Her bitch snarled in her mind, waiting impatiently for an opening where she could tear open Roderick's throat. Bailey hoped she got a chance.

Jaxon pushed up off the floor and stood in front of her. "Let her go," he valiantly said.

A chuckle that sent spidery shivers skating down

her spine made Roderick's eyes glow even brighter. "Aren't you still just the comedian? Stand aside, boy. You've completed your task for the moment. I won't be needing you now until the bitch whelps. And wasn't that kind of you to bind her to you before I had a chance to order it."

"What do you want with us?" Bailey demanded, standing to face her captor, trying to still the trembling of her limbs.

"I want my own pack, of course. One not bound to me by force but because they're mine. Born and bred for one thing, to serve me."

"You're sick."

"I prefer to think of myself as a visionary. And you should thank me. As the mother of the future ranks, you get to live, along with the pup here who so kindly brought you. I'm sure he'll be more than happy to play stud."

"Never," Jaxon growled.

"Really?"

Roderick never moved, but a moment later, Jaxon dropped to his knees, screaming as he clutched his head.

"Stop it!" Bailey cried.

"Why? The sooner he learns my will is the only one he should own, the better."

An alarm sounded, startling them all. Roderick's face creased, and his eyes went blank. Jaxon stopped screaming but still knelt on the floor, heaving. Sensing their chance, Bailey grabbed at him and pulled. He stumbled to his feet, but as she went to go around Roderick, his hand shot out and grabbed her arm in a painful grip.

"Going somewhere?"

Bailey tugged but got nowhere, and when Jaxon made to lunge at Roderick, he stopped halfway with a scream, clutching at his head instead.

"Come, my pets, it's time to leave. It would seem my son and his ragtag rabble of dogs have stumbled upon us."

As Roderick dragged her down a corridor lit by bulbs strung on a string, she couldn't help a bubble of hope.

Her mates had come for her.

* * * *

Parker chafed at the delay in following the signal left by Bailey as Jaxon, the traitor, took her farther and farther from the pack.

Not usually a rash man, he was ready to jump in his truck and go, but even among bloodthirsty werewolves, some preparation needed to happen. First off, the women and children left behind required protection, so some males were selected to stay and the females armed with guns. Sexist, but then again, a smaller female wolf didn't stand much of a chance against a larger aggressive male. Bullets, however, evened the odds.

Once they'd squared that situation away, they ran

into another. Nathan feared them leaving in a large group would alert Roderick's spies, so they slipped from the compound in vehicles that seemed empty except for drivers but were, in fact, packed with Lycans. The overflow of males ended up disgorging in towns on the way, picking up rental vehicles, dispersing their trail even more and making them less of a target if cops pulled them over. The whole process to get them on the road and en route to save Bailey took hours, and Parker could only stew in frustration, worrying about what had happened to his mate. As for Jaxon, the pack brother who'd taken her? The traitor wouldn't live long enough to regret betraying them.

A part of Parker understood that Jaxon probably hadn't acted of his own volition. It didn't matter. They could no longer trust him. Could no longer accept him into the fold of their pack. Even if they defeated Roderick, Parker knew the carefree boy he'd come to know would leave forever.

The drive lasted far longer than Parker liked, but his consolation resided in the fact that, while Bailey's captor drove, nobody could spare the time to harm her.

He knew the lack of sensation through their mating bond didn't bother him alone. The assumption was Roderick had done something to block the link they had with her. Or so they hoped. *I'd know if she was dead.*

When the GPS signal inside Bailey finally

stopped moving, they were still at least an hour behind with daylight fading fast, and Parker couldn't help the way he kept cracking his knuckles, needing to do something with the frantic energy flooding him. Gavin, behind the wheel for this last stretch, peered at him in the rearview.

"She's going to be fine."

"Of course she is," Wyatt snapped. "Bailey's a fighter."

Parker didn't reply. He knew Bailey would fight. He just hated she had to.

Arriving at their destination, only hours from where Gavin had first met their mate in the bar, they poured out of the truck and silently stripped. By unspoken decree, having arrived at least fifteen minutes ahead of everyone else, they opted to go in using stealth before the rest of the pack arrived. Nathan had made plans to go in when the sun rose, assuming his father would be resting, as the vampiric legends claimed. However, dawn still remained too many hours away. None of them could sit by idly for that amount of time while Bailey possibly suffered.

For once Parker embraced the pain of his change because the pain meant strength and speed, and he would need every ounce of it to save his woman.

Off they ghosted into the woods, luck on their side, as the wind kept them downwind of any patrolling rogues.

Still, the first sentry they killed raised the alarm, and the noisy distraction, while sadly announcing their infiltrating presence, did come with a bonus. Their link to Bailey was suddenly restored. With Roderick's attention wandering, probably rallying his troops, it allowed Parker and the others a beacon to locate Bailey.

Or not. They converged on a spot in the woods, no different than any other, overgrown with trees and shrubs. Parker's beast whined as it pawed at the ground, sensing Bailey but not seeing her.

She's underground, and moving. Arriving at the only possible conclusion, he kept his ears perked for sound, his nose sifting the myriad scents on the night breeze, and followed the link. He spotted the vehicle first, a dark sedan parked at the end of a path comprised of mashed-down weeds. Past it, the woods opened up but only for about twenty yards before dropping off, a deep gorge slicing through the earth, the rushing sound of water coming up to him.

In this clearing also stood a concrete cistern, and as he watched, the hatch on it lifted. Jaxon stumbled out first, quickly followed by Bailey and finally Roderick. Parker could only watch in cold fury—and heart-stopping fear—as Roderick grabbed Bailey by the throat, the sharp points of his claws digging into her alabaster skin. At his feet, Jaxon knelt, his head bowed. The dirty traitor. He would not leave these woods alive.

First, though, they'd need to fight because Roderick wasn't alone. From the stone well poured wolves, dozens of them, their hackles raised and their gums peeled back over their lips.

Parker braced himself, but the rogues did not immediately attack. A chilling laughter floated to him as Roderick, one hand still braced around Bailey's neck, pointed at them.

"So nice of you to join us," Roderick hissed.

"Let her go, Roderick. There is no escape," Gavin ordered, having shifted back to his human shape. Only their many years of friendship allowed Parker to recognize the terror he fought to hide.

"Look, my incubator, your dogs have arrived and are already barking orders. Shall I take them as I've taken your other lover?"

"No. Leave them alone," she cried, a reply to which the vampire tightened his grip, puncturing her flesh until rivulets of red ran down her skin.

"I'm going to kill you," Wyatt shouted, also forgoing his beast to speak.

Roderick laughed. "I've faced death before, numerous times, I might add. Apparently, that lord of darkness has no use for me because I'm still here. And keep in mind, if you try anything, the first to go will be your precious mate."

A red haze descended over Parker's gaze when the vampire's hand tightened around Bailey's throat, transforming the fear in her eyes to panic as she struggled to breathe.

"Bastard," Gavin whispered.

"Is that any way to speak to your master?"

Roderick replied. "Kneel for me, dogs. Bow to me, and maybe I'll let you live and serve."

"Never," Wyatt vowed.

"Funny, your friend here once said that. Shall I show you how I taught him to serve his master?"

Parker wondered at Roderick's words until the tenebrous touch of something cold and dark skittered at the edges of his mind.

Like hell. Nathan had warned them of Roderick's ability to control minds, and while the weak couldn't fight his touch—nor his son, bound to him by blood—the strong could. Parker pushed back at the crawling sensation, and judging by the grimace on Roderick's face, he wasn't the only one.

And that didn't please the vampire abomination at all. "Kill them," he screamed. "Kill them all!"

"No."

The word traveled to them on a whisper, and a puzzled glance at Gavin showed his pack mate just as confused. A flurry of movement made Wyatt's jaw drop, and Parker's heart swell in pride, even as his feet moved to bring him closer to help.

Jaxon, the strain on his face evident, sprang up from his crouch and half shifted, a true wolf man like Hollywood had never imagined.

"Down, dog!" Roderick bellowed.

Jaxon kept moving, his mouth opening and releasing a mournful howl imbued with a gut-wrenching agony. But Jaxon didn't stop, despite his evident pain, and sank his teeth into the vampire's arm. The hand holding Bailey released, and she slumped to the ground as Jaxon grappled with Roderick.

While the battle for supremacy took place, from the woods poured wolves, dozens of them, the pack arrived to join the fray, Nathan at their head. The rogues, confused by their leader's lack of direction, remained cognizant enough to know the newcomers were a threat and attacked.

Parker leapt over the thrashing furry bodies, his goal lying on the other side. A snarling wolf intercepted him, and Parker fought to keep gnashing teeth from his neck. Disposing of the rogue, he turned back to his objective.

As if in slow motion, he saw Wyatt and Gavin reach Bailey's side just as the wrestling duo edged toward the precipice. Roderick began to gain the upper hand, his mental power crushing Jaxon, who lost his wolf shape and screamed, "I love you, Bailey. Tell them all I'm sorry." And with those words, he bellowed as he surged forward against the vampire, toppling them over the edge.

A hoarse scream came from Bailey as Gavin dove forward, his fingers grasping for a hold of Jaxon. They met fabric . . . and tore free. A shocked silence followed that even the cacophony of battle couldn't interrupt. It lasted until the first of Bailey's harsh sobs.

The moment of freezing passed, and Wyatt scooped her into his arms as Gavin turned around to stroke a hand across her cheek.

"It's over, darling," he murmured.

"But Jaxon . . ." she wailed.

"Did what he had to, to redeem himself. For that, he will always be honored."

The battle, however, still went on. The rogues, even without their master, fought tooth and nail, although a crazy few did scurry over the edge of the cliff to join their sick lord in death. Parker had lost his thirst for battle, though. He accompanied Gavin and Wyatt as they strode with their mate back to their SUV, knowing their pack held the upper hand and would take care of the mess.

A heavy pall hung over them, the pitiful hiccup of Bailey's sobs the only sound as they traveled back. Parker drove as Gavin rocked her in the back. Wyatt sat shotgun, his face blankly peering out the window at the passing scenery only slowly lightening as day arrived.

"Pull over."

"Huh?" Parker dazedly came to himself and turned into the motel he assumed Wyatt meant. The thought of a long shower and a soft bed held a lot of appeal, anything to wipe away the gritty eyes and fatigue that pulled at him now that the adrenaline had worn off.

Idling at the front of the motel office, he waited for Wyatt to come back with a key. He parked in front of the last room on the row, and like battle-weary soldiers, they filed in, Bailey still nestled in

Gavin's arms.

He took her straight into the bathroom, and soon the sound of the shower came to them. Gavin returned, rubbing his face. "What a fucking night."

"Will she be okay?" Wyatt asked gruffly.

"She's tougher than she looks," Parker said.

The room held a pair of double beds, and Parker lay down on one, figuring he'd catch a few winks until his turn with the shower arrived.

Wyatt settled beside him with a gruff, "Keep your feet to yourself, or I'll make you into a midget."

"Try it, and I'll make you shriek like a little girl."

Their attempt at levity fell flat without Jaxon.

Parker closed his eyes but still heard the door when it opened and Bailey stepped out, her scent fresh and clean.

Gavin kissed her gently on the forehead. "I'm next," he said, and the door to the bathroom shut again before the shower pulsed.

Parker watched Bailey through hooded eyes, unsure if he should get up and do something or say something.

But what?

She stood surveying the beds, gnawing her lip. "Can we push them together?" Bailey's soft words saw him and Wyatt moving quickly to obey, sliding the heavy frames until the bed butted together, forming one massive sleeping surface.

A tired smile pulled at her lips. "Thanks. I don't want to be alone."

"I'm sorry," Wyatt whispered, saying what Parker longed to.

"For what?" she asked, appearing genuinely confused.

Parker hung his head. "We failed you. We said you would be safe, and you still got taken." The shame of it still made him burn.

"We don't deserve you," Wyatt added gruffly.

She approached them, raising her hands to stroke their cheeks. "You came for me. Just in the nick of time too. I'd call that the actions of heroes. And I'm the one who doesn't deserve you. If it weren't for me, none of you would have gotten caught up in that monster's plan, and Jaxon would still be alive." She broke then, sobbing, and he and Wyatt closed in on her, comforting her with softly spoken words and their bodies.

Wyatt swung her into bed and took to snuggling one of her sides while Parker took the other. When Gavin came out from the shower, he took Wyatt's place, comforting her. And when it came time for Parker to wash the grime of battle off, he did so, even though the water ran tepid.

When he returned, he found Bailey sleeping, the eyes of his brothers anxiously watching from either side. Parker slept at her feet, his arm thrown over her legs.

Despite her tears over Jaxon's demise, Parker couldn't help the relief that Bailey had survived. And even better, with Jaxon's last heroic act, Roderick was no more.

Chapter Seventeen

Waking up surrounded by male bodies proved interesting, especially when she needed to ease out to pee and brush her teeth. One of the guys had thought ahead and hit the motel's store because she found not only toothpaste and a brush but also some deodorant and lotion for her skin. The one thing she didn't bother with was clothes.

During her uneasy slumber, where she'd found herself sometimes crying, she'd taken time to reflect as the male bodies around her shifted positions but made sure to stay in close contact at all time.

She reflected on the fact that she had three men who cared so much for her that they faced down the ultimate in evil to save her. She mused on the growing wonder in her belly. And she rejoiced in the fact that she lived.

The loss of Jaxon would always be a wound in her psyche. Even without a bodily claim, she loved her fourth mate. Despite his demise, he would stay a part of her forever. But life went on. She'd had her moment to grieve and wail at the unfairness of the world, to ponder life's frail nature.

Now she needed to reaffirm her existence, to reignite the bonds that bound her with her lovers, her mates.

And what better way than through body-to-body, heart-pounding, skin-sweating sex.

Hence the naked body that sauntered out into the room, shocking her now woken and dressed men into silence. The dropped jaws were a nice touch.

Placing her hands on her hips, she eyed them with a saucy smile that was only slightly forced. "Now that I've finally got all three of my mates in one spot, albeit overdressed, I think it is long past time you all showed me just how well you share."

"What are you saying, darling?" Gavin asked cautiously, standing up from the chair.

She rolled her eyes. "I'm saying I want to feel alive. As in, I'm horny and I want all of you, pretty much at once, so what are we waiting for?" She couldn't quite manage her brazen words without a blush, but at least they worked. Clothes went flying, and in short order, she looked upon three utterly delicious naked men. *My men.*

Although they didn't say a word aloud, they seemed to own a plan of action as they moved in a seamless fashion that saw her placed on the bed, on her hands and knees, a very happy cock waving in her face.

A tanned hand stroked the hard dick, and she peered up at Wyatt, whose dark eyes danced with mischief.

"You asked for it, sunshine. I hope you can

handle it."

She didn't reply with words, not when she could let her tongue do the talking. She slid her lips over his silken head and down his length, caressing his skin as she went. She pulled on the prick, suctioning as she moved her way back up. A low moan came from him, but his wasn't the only rapid breathing.

Taking a look to her left, she saw Parker stroking his cock, a glazed look on his face. How decadent. A peek to the other side saw Gavin doing the same.

"I think we should see how good she is while distracted," said her blond cowboy.

The bed dipped as he moved behind her. Warm breath fluttered across her nether lips, and liquid heat pooled in her cleft. She bobbed her head, excitement filling her as she waited for the first touch. The mouth behind her teased, though, placing butterfly kisses on her inner thighs, blowing humidly onto her sex. It so distracted her that, when a hot mouth latched onto one of her hanging breasts, she jumped, clamping down on Wyatt's cock. His sharply drawn breath made her mumble an apology through her mouthful, but he didn't seem to mind, not if the way his cock throbbed in her mouth was any indication.

Keeping her rhythm proved hard with the mouth tugging and alternately biting down on her nipple. Add to that the mouth that finally latched onto her cleft, and she went still. Wyatt helped her out, his fingers threading through her hair and moving her up and down on his cock while the other two mouths lavished her with attention in an orgy of sensual delight.

A mewl forced itself past the object in her mouth when the torture on her clit subsided. And she let go of Wyatt's cock completely when Gavin's long prick thrust into her waiting wetness. Wyatt and Parker both shimmied out from under her, and she buried her face in the bedcover, her bottom pushed straight up as Gavin pumped into her, bringing her to the edge of bliss.

Then stopping. She cried out, craning to look back, and saw Gavin switch places with Wyatt, who, with a lift of a dark brow, slammed into her waiting pussy. She clawed at the fabric as his hard thrusts rocked her body, butting against her sensitive G-spot. She climbed the peak of pleasure even faster and hovered on its edge when he withdrew.

"No!" she yelled, her channel throbbing and begging for relief. But they had other plans.

Parker took his turn next, the thickness of his shaft stretching her, but unlike the previous two, he didn't piston. He took his time, languorously pushing into her, swirling then retreating. Over and over. Bailey could only keen at the intense sensation.

But slow and steady or not, his torture brought her to the brink. So, of course, he stopped, and Bailey almost cried. "Why are you doing this to me?"

"Doing what? Sharing?" Wyatt mocked.

"Isn't that what you asked for?" Gavin added.

"You know we serve to please," Parker finished.

"Make me come!" She managed to not scream it, but barely.

They flipped her onto her back. Parker and Wyatt each grabbed a leg and pulled it up and away, exposing her to Gavin's ardent gaze. His cock jutted proudly from his body, the tip of it gleaming. She arched her hips at him, silently begging.

With a melting smile, he sank into her, his gaze locked to hers. "I love you, Bailey," he whispered as he thrust into her, the walls of her sex clutching him tightly. "Forever and ever." Quickening his pace, he increased the friction, and yet, despite their frantic hip-rolling, they kept eye contact. They came together, the roaring wave of orgasm sweeping them and rushing through their bodies.

Before the quakes subsided, she found herself placed on Wyatt's lap, straddling him, his cock sliding into her wet sheath. He rubbed his rough cheek against hers as he rotated his hips, driving his cock into her still-quivering channel.

"Sunshine, you are my everything," he murmured against her ear as he clutched her to him tightly.

A body pressed in from behind, and a hand slid between their bodies to find her clit. The rubbing of her already sensitive nub as Wyatt bounced her on his lap soon had her second climax striking, the milking strength of it making Wyatt gasp as he shot his pleasure into her.

But it wasn't done. There still remained her

gentle giant to take care of.

He lay on his back, his hooded eyes watching as his brothers grabbed her with gentle hands and lowered her on his staff. Spent, Bailey wasn't quite sure how she could manage the strength to bring him off. She needn't have worried. Three sets of hands clasped her body, and a pair of mouths found her straining nipples. They rocked her slowly on Parker's cock, swirling her just right and hitting that delicious inner spot of hers.

"Oh, baby," her gentle giant rumbled. "There's no place I'd rather be than with you for the rest of my life."

Tears pricked, and she hoped her tremulous smile and shining eyes showed how much she loved him. Loved all of them.

Her third orgasm made her body seize, her muscles tightening for so long she thought she'd keel over with the intensity of it. When her body finally released, it took her breath and the rest of her thoughts with it. A shudder wracked Parker's body as his hot seed joined the others in bathing her channel.

To think, a lifetime ago, she would have been appalled at a woman who would bed three men at a time. *Talk about missing out. I love my men, each and every one of them.* And according to pack law, mating was for life.

Lucky her.

Epilogue

Hugging her superbly large stomach, Bailey waddled to the front porch her mates had built her and surveyed them as they worked on their newest present to her—a gazebo. She still hadn't quite figured out what one did with that structure, but she didn't tell them that, not when they seemed so darned determined to give her one.

Next on their agenda, they'd informed her, was a play structure for the baby. Never mind the child wouldn't be big enough to play on it for at least a year or more. Apparently their child would need one. And the list went on.

Truly, though, she couldn't complain. How many women had three men determined to make her life as wonderful as possible? Sometimes she couldn't believe her luck, but as Dana, her best female friend, said, *"Three is so much better than one. Especially all at once."*

Absently, she ran her tongue over the inside of her bottom lip, the small, ridged scar from the small bite Jaxon had given her—their mating exchange—tingling again. She'd told the boys about her binding with Jaxon in the cell. They'd accepted it and then never spoken of it again. However, she found it harder than them to forget the man with the beautiful smile and dancing green eyes. She relived his death, his final words, over and over .

She dreamt of him sometimes, calling to her from some dark, painful place. She woke from those dreams sweating, allowing whichever man she slept with to comfort her.

What she didn't tell them was her belief that Jaxon lived—along with Roderick. Truthfully, she was pretty sure they already suspected, given the way they never let her out of sight and the way the security for the compound never abated, even after that final battle.

She knew one day Roderick, that evil creature, would return, but this time, she'd be prepared for him. The pack would eventually have their revenge.

In the meantime, she would live life to the fullest with her mates. She would birth her child and become a mother. And most of all, she would love.

Stepping down from the porch, she'd barely hit the grass when the hum of male voices surrounded her, along with their musky scent. She let their enthusiasm and affection roll over her, feeling the baby kick in response.

In that moment, she believed, that no matter what the future held, they would prevail—and be happy.

Forever.

The End

Next story: Seeking Pack Redemption

www.ingramcontent.com/pod-product-compliance
Lightning Source LLC
LaVergne TN
LVHW021052100526
838202LV00083B/5515